REFERENCE LIBRARY

SHROPSHIRE COUNTY
LIBRARY

This book ...
REFERENCE (..... ...d
must not be taken out of
the building.

THE HOUSE IN THE LANE

Celia and Larry married after only a brief courtship, yet she would have said that he was so transparent, and she loved him so well, that she could read his very thoughts. But after they settled in The Red House— the old house which he had insisted on buying against his mother's strenuous opposition—Celia began to wonder. Why was Larry so preoccupied? How was it that she had no idea what was worrying him? Was she only imagining that people in the village shops were looking at her oddly? She told herself that the loneliness in the daytime was getting on top of her. Then, one evening, there came a knocking at the back door . . .

The House in the Lane

by

WINIFRED MANTLE

ROBERT HALE & COMPANY
63 Old Brompton Road, London S.W.7

© *Winifred Mantle 1972*

First published in Great Britain 1972

ISBN 0 7091 2348 5

PRINTED IN GREAT BRITAIN BY
BRISTOL TYPESETTING CO. LTD.
BARTON MANOR - ST. PHILIPS
BRISTOL

ONE

YOU WON'T ask Larry where the blue rabbit went, Celia told herself. You made up your mind yesterday evening that you never would. Half an hour ago you reminded yourself that it wouldn't be a clever thing to do. You're not a moron; when you know that you've been thinking of doing a silly thing, and you decide not to do it, you don't do it.

So she tried to approach the subject by a roundabout route.

"Did you enjoy your dinner?" she said; and had to add, "Larry!" for her husband seemed not to have heard her.

He looked vaguely down at his plate, where the stew had left a brown smear.

"Yes. Yes, thank you," he said.

"Really?" Celia asked brightly. "Is that how you like your dumplings? Is that how your mother made them, when you were young?"

Larry looked at her as if he had just woken up. "I suppose so," he said. "But she didn't make dumplings, ever, as it happens. So I can never say to you, this isn't as good as Mother made, can I? You're safe from that."

" Yes, that's something," replied Celia, and managed to laugh with him.

The approach, by way of childhood, and childish things, had been much too roundabout.

" I'll wash up; you read the paper," Celia said.

Larry agreed. She knew that it was not because he had had a hard day at the office, nor because in six weeks of marriage he had grown tired of helping with the housework. It was because he didn't want to talk. She glanced at him from time to time as she went in and out clearing the table. He spent a full minute staring blankly at the evening paper in just the way he had stared at his empty plate. Then he collected himself, and settled down to read.

Celia dumped the dirty crockery on the copper-board of the vast old-fashioned scullery. Usually she liked the scullery, which she was just beginning to think of as hers. It was whitewashed, with red quarries on the floor, and the stove stood in a huge cavernous alcove where the old range had been removed. But this evening she hardly saw the room, or felt its fireless chill. She was remembering.

Celia had worn white and gold at her wedding. She had looked radiant. Larry, on the other hand, had been stiff as a guardsman on parade. The touch of a finger, one felt, and he would fall flat on his face in a faint. Celia could hear her family whispering to each other. Who would have thought it of Larry Riddell? they asked; he normally seemed so endearingly at ease, and interested in his surroundings.

When the service was over, Celia's brother, Steve, who was best man, was moved by Larry's set face to make one of the routine jokes. It was something quite innocuous —" Cheer up, it's the first time that's the worst, you know "—something like that—but Larry turned on him in a way Celia would never have believed possible. Fortunately Steve was understanding.

" Man, are your nerves in a state! " he said forgivingly. He began to be funny about a disturbance there had been in church—an old woman who had suddenly stood up and said something unintelligible, and then seemed to realise where she was, and hurried out. As the interruption had come just after the vicar said the bit about any impediment, one or two people were laughing about the shock it had very nearly given them. But Celia, who was used to reassuring younger brothers and sisters who had exams to face or interviews to go through, steered Larry away from the facetious. He realised what she was doing, and once he gave her a shamefaced smile.

" Don't take any notice of Steve," he said. " My nerves are all right. I wanted the service over, that's all. Now we can relax."

But it was not till they were driving off, and the family, calling and waving, fell back out of sight, that Larry let out a satisfied breath.

" Did you hate it?" Celia asked. " I suppose my family in the mass is overwhelming."

Larry had only his mother, whose arthritis had been too bad for her to attend the ceremony, though she had sent a long and loving telegram. Larry had invited three friends from the estate agent's office where he worked, but Celia's noisy brothers and sisters, as well as her parents and aunts and uncles, had very much predominated. Still, Celia was bitterly disappointed that Larry had not enjoyed their wedding. But he reassured her.

" I like your family," he said simply. " I'm sorry if

I seemed dull, but, to be honest, I was longing for it to be over."

He added, as the car swung round at the sign ' Airport ', " And, in case you don't know, I'd go through it again three times over, for you."

It was a second afterwards that Celia found the anonymous letter.

It was on a cheap sheet of paper, not folded, not addressed or signed, and it must have been placed on the seat of the car at some time while it was waiting empty at the door. Celia had swept it towards the armrest when she got in, and now, feeling for her handbag, her fingers happened across it. She smiled. It was probably a good luck note from one of the children, she thought.

Larry was preoccupied with the road. Celia refrained from calling his attention, as she had thought of doing. She glanced at the message.

It read, "I hope you remember every day and every night the poor girl you ought to be marrying."

TWO

FOR A second Celia couldn't take it in. Then her immediate reaction was to hide the letter from Larry. She thrust it into her bag, and took out her lipstick at the same time, so that he should not notice the movement. With hands that trembled a little she pretended to be retouching her lips. The shock was enormous. In her happy life she had never had an anonymous letter, never known malice from someone unnamed. It was the anonymity and spite which terrified and sickened her. She did not for one instant consider the idea that whoever wrote it might have reason on her side. Larry had not jilted another girl, or got one into trouble, she knew that as a fact. The insinuation was the invention of a demented mind. Celia's only concern was that Larry should never learn about it.

She was lucky. Larry was thinking about the plane, the hotel, whether they would like Majorca when they got there. He must have seen Celia pick up the note, but it did not occur to him to ask what it was. To Celia it seemed to be burning a hole in her bag; and she would not have been surprised if the airport police, seeing her guilty look, had arrested her on sight. But Larry noticed nothing.

Actually, they did enjoy Majorca. Celia had formed no clear idea of what to expect from her honeymoon, except blazing sun and the happiness of belonging to each other, and she had some surprises. Larry asked a lot of her, and saw that he got it, sweetly, but imperiously, as of right. At first Celia was inclined to laugh at his ardour, and be tolerant, but presently all her detachment faded as she was caught up in a heightened awareness and love of him that she would never had believed she could attain.

In this mood, nothing else seemed to matter, and it was with perfect unconcern that, coming across the anonymous letter crumpled with a forgotten bus-ticket in her bag, she crushed them up together, and put them in the waste-paper-basket.

It was a September morning when they had to return to England. They went out on a last-minute shopping excursion, to get rid of their remaining currency. Celia spent hers on a miniature olivewood carving which Larry had admired, and which would remind them, she hoped, of Majorca. Larry did not tell her what he had bought, and when she was doing their packing she placed several small wrapped parcels in his suitcase without being able to satisfy her curiosity.

The parcels were in gay striped paper, but they were not all very secure. Celia was sure she had had nothing to do with it, yet she felt quite guilty when one of them came partly undone, and revealed a corner. She took a peep, and was consumed with astonishment. There was no mistaking what she was looking at. It was a small fluffy blue rabbit, the sort one can buy anywhere where there are baby-shops, certainly not typically Spanish, probably made in England. Who was Larry intending it for, she wondered. He had only his mother. There had been various children whom his mother had fostered, Celia knew, but they were all grown-up and scattered.

Celia had never heard Larry mention any young god-children. Surely he did not intend the rabbit as a present for one of Celia's sisters? The youngest, Rosemary, was twelve, and even a man unused to children could not suppose that Rosemary would welcome a fluffy blue rabbit as a mascot.

It was a mystery. Celia nearly asked Larry about it. If he had been in the room, she certainly would have done. But he was out on the balcony, and she remembered in time that he had said nothing to her about the purchase, nor attempted to show it to her. It was meant to be a secret, and so, though she marvelled, she tucked the rabbit back in the striped paper, closed the case, and told Larry that they were ready.

From the sun and the beaches, the mountains, and the fishing-boats, Larry and Celia were going to a house on the fringe of a Staffordshire industrial town, hours away from Celia's home. For Larry, it meant also a new job, though he, unlike Celia, had lived in the district before, Celia had only seen the house for one snatched week-end, and was looking forward to getting to work on it; but she had not understood the change there would be in her way of life.

She had been used to the cosy intimacy of a small office, the comings and goings of a large family. She had had no idea that being alone in a house, even one's own, could be so depressing. Larry did not come home at lunch-time, and in the evening he was often later than she expected, for he was determined to make a good impression on his new firm.

Celia had plenty to occupy herself with, of course. She was painting all the walls of the house—Larry did the ceilings at week-ends—and freeing the garden from the tangle of weeds. But even the satisfaction of seeing flowers emerge where there were none before, and of having clean bright rooms instead of drab ones, was not enough, she discovered, to make up for the loneliness. She longed for Larry's return, almost as soon as he had set out, and then, when he did arrive, he was tired and disinclined to look at what she had done until he had rested. Celia was patient. She understood that Larry was working for their future. But she was on the verge of deep unhappiness, only a month after life had seemed ecstatic.

When she felt that she would go mad unless she saw a

human face, Celia used to take the quarter of an hour's walk down the lane into the village. There, at least, people answered her when she spoke, though they were sometimes so long about it that she was afraid they meant to ignore her. And they smiled when she smiled, though warily. They were not hostile, she told herself, just cautious of the stranger. And while she agreed that it was understandable, and that she had only to be patient to find that she was accepted, at times she had the feeling that in going to live at The Red House, which was seventy years old, she had gone back seventy years, when to move to a place in which one had not been born, was to be an object of suspicion and hate.

It was the loneliness, Celia was sure, that put her in mind again, and so often, of the anonymous letter. But it was the Devil himself, she was convinced, that made her connect the letter with the blue rabbit. Though all Larry's other parcels had been produced, and proved to be intended for herself, or for his mother, the package with the blue rabbit had simply disappeared. Celia searched Larry's belongings for it, and so confirmed that it was no longer in the house. Yet she dared not simply ask him what he had done with it. She understood his every smile and frown, she was sure she could predict how he would react to questions about love and life, religion and politics, or whether they should have potted shrimps for Sunday tea. But she did not know how he would take it if she asked him what he had done with the blue rabbit, and she was afraid to put it to the test.

THREE

CELIA FINISHED washing and drying, and put the china away in the low narrow pantry, a step down from the scullery. There wasn't a light in there. That was one of the things they were going to attend to. She and Larry had great plans for this house. Celia liked the high ceilings and large rooms, and didn't mind the steep stairs and the scarcity of power points. It was because of such disadvantages, after all, that The Red House had been cheap enough for Larry to be able to buy.

She went back into the living-room. The fire, which she always built up to welcome Larry home at night, was roaring cheerfully. The old hide armchair they had bought for five shillings at the sale rooms received her into its hollow. Larry looked up, laid aside the paper, and said,

"What sort of a day did you have?"

Until this evening, Celia had been careful to be amusing over the trials of settling in—they had agreed that she should not get a job again until she had mastered the art of running an inconvenient house in a built-up village which had only a cluster of shops at the crossroads. But tonight there was a note of complaint in her voice that was new.

"Oh, the usual," she said. "The bread called, and the

milk, and a man to ask if he could pull down the old out-houses. Then I went to the shops. The old man at the corner was in his garden, as usual, and he stared at me, as usual, and his wife stared at me from behind her parlour curtain, as usual. And in the grocer's they all stopped talking and stared, and the same in the butcher's."

"You're new," said Larry.

"Oh, I know. But this place isn't a village any more. Look at The Red House. Three houses built on the old garden. There must be fifty new families who have moved into new houses round here in the last year or so. Why stare at me? I begin to think that there must be something extra peculiar about me."

"Of course there isn't," said Larry quickly.

He sounds as if he imagines I mean it, Celia thought.

"To be fair, they didn't stare in the cake-shop," she said.

"You see," said Larry, with undisguised relief.

"It's doing a lot of business. They've put on another girl, and they've only been open a month."

"Good," said Larry.

What does he mean by saying 'good' in that tone? thought Celia. What is it to us if a chain store makes a fortune out of its half-cooked buns and ghastly mock-cream cakes? She said,

"That's why they don't stare, I suppose. They're even newer than I am."

"It's only because you're someone fresh," Larry repeated.

He was making Celia feel as if there really was something peculiar about the way the old man at the corner, and his wife behind the curtain, and the manager of the grocer's, and of the butcher's, looked at her. Celia had sometimes thought there must be, but it was an idea she thrust aside. That was what people imagined when they were so lonely that they became mental, and she didn't intend to get that way.

" I wish you'd hurry the electrician," she said, suddenly peevish. " Then we could have our television."

" I'll get on to them again in the morning," Larry replied.

He was eager. He could still be eager about things like that. Celia was sorry she had sounded cross.

" Well, at least no one can interrupt us in our favourite programme," she said, stretching her toes in the warmth from the hearth.

Ask me what my favourite programme was, she willed him. After all, we only walked out together for eight weeks before we got married. We really know nothing about each other. Tell me about the other girl you might have married, and whether she asked you to bring back a mascot. There's hours and hours of lovely talking before us, while we find out about each other's past. But Larry was staring into the fire in his new abstracted style. Whatever he saw there was giving him no pleasure.

" I said ' no one can interrupt us in our favourite programme,' " Celia repeated.

" No. It's plain now that no one will just drop in," said Larry, in a disappointed voice.

On that, as if it was a cue, there came a knocking at the door.

It was the back door.

" I'll go," Larry said.

Celia followed him.

They crossed the scullery swiftly, not bothering to put on the light. The window over the sink, and the door to the living-room, not quite shut, faintly illumined their way. There was no more knocking; whoever was outside was waiting quietly.

Larry opened the door. Celia had just time to see a dim shape in the dusk, and to be sure that it was nothing frightening, not a thug nor a drunk, before the person who had been standing waiting slumped at Larry's feet.

It was a woman, a young woman. As she fell, her hat rolled off, and bowled a few paces into the room.

"Help her!" Celia exclaimed urgently, and bent to try to raise the stranger up again.

Larry moved Celia aside, and tugged the woman to her feet.

"Better get her to the fire," he suggested, breathing hard.

Celia ran to throw the inner door wide. The woman was able to walk, though her head was down on her chest. Half lifting, supporting her, Larry brought her to the fire and into the light.

Larry dumped the woman in Celia's chair, which was the nearer, and stood back, waiting for her to recover. Being jolted out of his abstraction suited him. He looked boyishly excited. Celia, holding the stranger's smart little hat in her hand, stood silently looking on.

The woman's head had fallen back; her eyes were closed. She had a sharp face, well-featured, and, at the moment, a bad colour; her hair was dark and naturally curly; she looked to Celia to be about thirty years old. Celia had never set eyes on her before; nor, she imagined, from the way he was absorbing every feature, had Larry. They waited a second or two. Celia thought of tea, but did not move to make it. She did not want to miss anything.

The woman sighed, opened her eyes, which were a vivid blue, and straightened a little in the chair. Colour came back into her face, and made her instantly several years younger.

" I'm sorry," she muttered.

She was respectable, by her voice, and by her dress, but without any of the new easy money. Celia decided this, and wondered what could have happened to her. Did they need a doctor, or police?

" Would you like a cup of tea?" she asked.

" Brandy," suggested Larry.

Celia hesitated. Hadn't Larry heard of women who went round pretending to faint, just for the sake of a few sips of brandy people offered them? But at the mention of brandy the stranger sat up again, sniffed, and said,

" You know I can't stand the smell of it."

You know? She must still be confused. But, reassured by the firmness of the tone, Celia ran for the tea-pot.

She had to stay in the scullery, boiling the kettle on the gas, putting the cup on the tray. Fortunately there was warm water left in the kettle from washing-up, and she was not away long. She could not hear voices, and when she got back into the sitting-room it was plain that no one had spoken since she left. Larry had sat down; the woman was resting, with a hand to her head.

She took the cup Celia offered her with a murmured ' Thank you.' The first sip restored her; Celia could see her spirit return. Perception came into her eyes, and strength into her backbone. She gave little glances at Larry.

" Are you ill?" Celia asked.

The woman's eyes considered her, in her turn.

"No," she replied slowly. "No, I'm not ill. I can't think what I was doing, fainting at the door. It was seeing someone I didn't expect, I suppose."

"Did you expect to see a friend?" asked Celia in astonishment. The Red House—red brick, stained glass lights, slate roof—was not like any of the bright modern villas which were now its neighbours. No one could mistake it for another house in the lane.

The woman frowned. Celia wondered whether she could be a mental patient. But when she spoke she sounded normally surprised at herself.

"I was in town," she said. "I had a shock there—a dreadful shock."

Her eyes clouded again as she spoke.

"I was knocked down," she explained. "Rolled into the gutter. Some man helped me up, and then rushed on. I never even thanked him, I remember, I was so confused. I don't know what got into me, then. Someone asked me where I wanted to go, and I told them, and they must have put me on the bus I said. I remember getting off at the crossroads, and thinking I'd only got a bit further to go, and then I should be all right. I don't remember walking down the lane. I got to the back door, but it wouldn't open, so I knocked. And then you came. It was a shock. Everything seemed to go round me. I suppose I'd been a bit more shaken-up than I thought . . ."

"But who were you expecting?" asked Celia. Nothing in her own and Larry's appearance could have upset the woman, obviously, but still she was a little offended.

"Well, you see, I thought I was coming home," was the answer. Celia stiffened. She did not trust people who claimed to have had lapses of memory. Larry did not seem to suspect anything, however. He did not speak.

"Home? Here?" Celia asked, glancing at him for support.

"I was born here," the woman said. "I lived here till I went away to work. You've cut the big cherry-tree down."

"That was done when they took the garden for building," explained Celia. "You've lived here? Then your family must have been here before the old man that we bought from, I suppose."

"Mr. Yates. He bought The Red House when my grandmother and grandfather died. He was an old man, then, and his wife was older. So he hung on all these years, did he? He let the place go down."

"We shall try to get it into shape again," put in Larry, apologising.

"Your name must be Belmont, then, mustn't it?" pursued Celia. "It was the Belmonts who were here before Mr. Yates."

"My name was Belmont, Iris Belmont. It's Iris Anslow now. I married. I'd have done better not to." She looked at Larry, a bold brazen look which startled Celia.

"I'm sorry," said Larry, like a polite child.

"Would you like a biscuit with your tea, Mrs. Anslow?" Celia put in, embarrassed.

"I won't eat your biscuits," Iris Anslow replied.

It was the way local people still spoke. The implication was not that the biscuits might be poisonous, Celia knew. It was a formula, she had concluded, left over from the days when abject poverty was the rule, and you didn't take from people food they needed themselves, though politeness had led them to suggest it. Mrs. Anslow was telling the truth when she claimed to be a local woman.

" Another cup of tea, then?" said Celia.

" If there's one in the pot," replied Iris.

FOUR

CELIA POURED out again. She looked questioningly at Larry, but he shook his head. So Iris Anslow drank her second cup of tea alone, staring into the fire. Larry remembered to get up and give Celia his armchair. He drew up a dining-chair between her and Mrs. Anslow, and they all sat in silence.

When Iris handed the empty cup back to him, Larry spoke.

" You can't not have recognised me," he stated, to Celia's amazement.

" Oh, no, you're Larry Riddell, all right." This time Iris's look was dull—Celia relaxed.

" This is my wife, Celia," Larry said.

Mrs. Anslow glanced at Celia, but made no comment.

" You must still know a lot of people around here," Larry went on.

" I suppose so," replied Iris, unenthusiastically.

" The place has changed a lot," said Larry.

" It has," Iris replied.

Did Larry think it would help Mrs. Anslow to talk about the old days in which they had obviously met, Celia wondered. Well, why not? Mrs. Anslow must have had concussion, surely, to forget where she was bound for, and make for her old home? But when people had concussion, didn't they forget the accident, too? Obviously not. In any case, there was no hurry. Celia and Larry had had nothing in view, except staining a bedroom floor, and it was cold upstairs in this cold autumn.

" How many houses were there in the lane in the old days?" Larry asked. " Eight or nine? I don't remember."

" More like seven," replied Iris. " Let's see; there'd be the Hands, the Wards, the Baileys, the Fletchers, and one or two more, well spaced-out, of course."

" And now there are fifty or so!" said Celia.

" But the new houses aren't a patch on this," said Iris jealously. " Nor the other old ones weren't, either, of course. The Red House was much the best house in the lane."

And was still not everyone's cup of tea, Celia thought. Indeed, Larry's mother had been horrified at the idea of Larry buying The Red House. She said it would ruin him in repairs. But Larry decided otherwise. Mrs. Riddell had been so outspoken, however, that he had not let her know that he was negotiating to buy. He had presented her with a *fait accompli*. She hadn't liked it. She was a headstrong, outspoken, managing woman, even at sixty, even half crippled with arthritis. But it had been too late for anything she said to have any effect.

" What has happened to the other families in the lane?" Larry was asking.

The quick look Iris gave him was full of suspicion.

Why, she isn't quite sure about us, Celia thought, with a positive shock. I've been sitting here wondering about her, whether she's right in the head, and whether she could make herself a nuisance by staying too long, and she must have been sitting there wondering about us. Is it only doubt whether we are going to chop any more of the old trees down, and put in extra windows? Or does she think we might snatch her handbag, something like that?

Larry too, had noticed the suspicion. He spoke coaxingly, and more specifically.

" The Baileys—what happened to them?" he asked.

" I heard they opened a butcher's," answered Iris.

And they stare at new customers, thought Celia.

" And the Wards?"

" The grocer's," said Celia.

" They have the grocer's then, the way they always used to," nodded Iris, with more animation. " A little general shop in their front room, just the one window, it used to be when I was young. But everybody round here has gone up in the world."

Larry was about to continue the list. Celia interrupted.

" And what's the name of the old couple who live in the corner cottage, the old one with the big garden?" she asked. They made the third group of starers; which was the reason for her intervention.

Iris Anslow stiffened. She stiffened like a snake rearing its head. Celia could feel the animosity. She felt her own spine go rigid, as if she were a cat putting up her back at the snake. The silence lasted a good half minute. Then Iris replied.

" Their name is Anslow, like mine. I should have thought you knew."

" Oh, no," babbled Celia. " We've only been here six weeks, and nobody has mentioned the name. I never see them to talk to, of course, but just call ' Good morning ' sometimes as I go by to the shops."

" Bill Anslow would say good morning to anybody. He's so good-natured he's soft," observed Mrs. Anslow.

In face of this judgment it was difficult to know how to ask, Is he any relation? And, of course, he must be. The name could not be a coincidence.

Iris put an end to Celia's silent speculation.

" I ought to know. He's my husband," she said. " I'm the only Mrs. Anslow there is here."

"But there's a Mrs. Bill Anslow, isn't there? She can't be his mother! I was sure they were husband and wife," said Celia.

Iris smiled. " You're not the only one," she stated.

" Isn't she Mrs. Anslow?" demanded Celia.

" No. She calls herself that. I don't know what she signs herself when she has to sign her name. But there's one thing—she'll be buried as Miss Flora Belmont. She won't be able to call herself Mrs. Anslow then."

Iris spoke as if this was a fact which gave her a certain satisfaction.

" Belmont?" Celia queried. " Did you say Belmont?"

" She's my aunt. I should have thought you knew," said Iris again.

" No, I didn't know that," Larry replied. He seemed dazed, and Celia could not blame him. She felt disconcerted, herself. It was a situation where even an expert on etiquette might have been at a loss for the right word.

Larry apparently decided to deal with the matter by changing the subject.

"You know this house better than we do," he observed. "There have been times when we should have been glad of someone who did. The garden, for instance. I tried a little digging, and soon found that I was throwing out bulbs. We shall have to wait now till we see where they come up. And, inside the house . . . Mr. Yates lived alone, and his married daughter hardly knew the place. There was no one to tell me where the hot water pipes ran, and the plumbers didn't seem to be able to work it out. In the end they had to get one of the bedroom floors up. Just to have a look."

"They would. But I couldn't help you," said Iris. "Many a time I watched Gran tie the ballcock up, to stop the tank running over, that sort of thing. But I don't think she ever knew which way pipes ran under the floor. That was my Grandad's business. He expected Gran and Aunt Flora and my mother to work as hard as men, but he didn't thank a woman for knowing anything he didn't need her to know."

"He sounds rather a martinet; they all were, in those days, I suppose," said Larry.

"He had them afraid to draw breath in case it didn't suit his idea for them. He wouldn't be able to do it now," returned Iris.

They sat for a moment in silence.

"Well?" said Celia, breaking it. She was looking at Iris, wondering whether it was not time the guest offered to make a move.

Iris must have known what Celia meant, but she sat on. Celia's premonition of trouble returned in force. She was about to say something definite about Larry seeing Mrs. Anslow on her way, or perhaps to a doctor, when there was another interruption. There came another knocking on the door, this time loud and frenzied.

All three heads turned towards it. It seemed to Celia that Iris Anslow was the least surprised.

" Someone in a hurry," she observed complacently. " Hadn't you better answer it?"

But there was no need. Whoever it was had opened the back door, and was blundering through the scullery towards the light under the living-room door.

FIVE

CELIA ROSE to her feet. Iris Anslow, in contrast, planted herself more deeply in her armchair. Larry got up and went to the door and threw it open. Then he said, " Oh, hullo," in a baffled voice, and stepped back into the living-room.

" Come in," he said politely, and made a gesture towards the fire, allowing Celia to see who the visitor was.

It was the man from the corner house. Without his gardening cap he did not look quite so old. Or else it was that Celia felt he couldn't be more than twenty years older than his wife, who had glanced round, and then turned her face back to the fire, ignoring him.

Bill Anslow was extremely agitated. He gave a little nod

at Celia, acknowledging her presence, but then turned to Iris without further pretence at politeness.

" Iris! " he said. " What are you doing here! What have you come back for?"

"What a way to behave!" she reprimanded him. "Do you always come pushing into other folks' houses without so much as a by-your-leave, and without even saying good evening?"

Bill Anslow looked ludicrously baffled and frustrated. Celia could believe that he was too gentle to get angry, but he was nearly bursting with indignation and anxiety. He spluttered, achieving no speech.

" How did you know I was here?" Iris asked.

" Flora saw you from the window. She saw you get off the bus and start down the lane. She knew it was you. It was you! "

"Of course it was me. Nobody's denied it," said Iris, with good-natured contempt. " I was just wondering how Aunt Flora recognised me in the dark after all these years. But that lamp must be a god-send to anyone who wants to watch who's getting on and off the bus. She wouldn't know what to do with herself, without it, I expect. Nothing to think about."

"Don't you start on Flora, now," Bill Anslow warned her. But it was a feeble protest. He knew it would have no effect.

" I've no hard words to say about Aunt Flora," returned Iris. " Some people might say I had good cause to, but she's taken nothing off me that I wasn't better without. At least, I don't think she has. I shall find out, if she did, you tell her from me."

" What do you mean?"

" Never you mind. You'd better take yourself off. And apologise, too, I should, while you're about it, for coming rushing in here, and making a row. What will Larry Riddell think?"

Larry and Celia were standing consciously to one side, letting the drama unfold itself without their participation. There seemed nothing else to do. Larry gave a start, as Iris looked meaningly at him. He murmured foolishly,

" It doesn't matter."

" Not at all," said Celia.

Bill Anslow stood irresolute.

" You'd better be getting back to Aunt Flora. She never could bear to be left alone in the house," said Iris.

It was like telling a dog to go home: and Bill Anslow, like a dog, began to obey. Larry went into the scullery to put the light on for him. About to follow, Bill spoke to Celia.

" It couldn't be the same family as Zelda Riddell?" he said.

" My husband's mother's name is Griselda," admitted Celia.

" I didn't know," said Bill Anslow, in an apologetic voice. " We hadn't heard that Zelda Wright's son was back. We knew she was married, of course. She wouldn't have more than the one, I suppose?"

" No," said Celia.

" No," agreed Mr. Anslow. " Laurie Riddell was killed just as the fighting stopped."

The memory seemed to subdue him. He murmured good night, and went to the door.

" Did you know Mrs. Riddell, too, then?" asked Celia of Iris.

" Oh, yes. We all knew her," answered Iris.

" She remembered this house," said Celia.

" I should think she would remember it! " exclaimed Iris. " When she was a child she spent more time in it than in her own, Aunt Flora used to say."

Larry came back from the scullery, and looked from one to the other.

" Mrs. Anslow was just telling me that she knew your mother in the old days," said Celia brightly.

" Mom hardly ever mentions the old days," explained Larry, his face eager.

He was anxious to talk about his mother to Iris Anslow, thought he had never seemed to consider that Celia might be curious about his childhood. That hurt Celia, but she told herself not to be absurd. She schooled herself to listen, while Iris and Larry talked.

How Larry talked! He was apparently keenly interested in every aspect of life in the lane in his mother's day, and Iris Anslow, in a curt way, was forced to satisfy him. There emerged a picture of the seven or so families, a little community isolated from the town by the scrappy bus service —one bus every half hour at peak times—and served by its one little grocer's shop. The heads of families in the lane were not countrymen—they were townsmen by birth, every one of them, with jobs in the town. But they had all kept hens, and grown vegetables, and some of them had kept pigs and bees, as well.

Reading between the lines, Celia thought she had a right to be sorry for Flora, and Maud Belmont, and the young women reared in the lane. They had apparently worked in offices all day, and then gone back to town after tea, to spend at least three of their evenings at night school.

At home they were expected to dig, and feed animals, as well as cook, and make their own clothes. If they wanted to go to a theatre they had to walk five miles home afterwards—there was no late bus—and there were very few youths whose ardour did not wilt at the idea of having to see them home. Fortunately there had also been some young men among the families in the lane.

Then the war came, and it all disintegrated. People who had never expected to travel more than a mile or two from their homes, to settle there into much the same life as their parents, were removed to the ends of the earth, literally, and not one in a dozen came back.

Learning so much about Iris Anslow and her relations, Celia also learned something about her husband. His extraordinary persistence impressed and amused her. She was struck by his familiarity with the lane. Of course she had realised that he knew The Red House well by sight. He had told her that his mother used to bring him by bus to walk up and down the lane, and then to take the bus home again, as soon as he could walk so far. Now he spoke of passing by on his bicycle during the school holidays. Celia imagined it had been a private ambition of his to live in The Red House when he grew up. Well, he had achieved it, but, in the way these things happen, The Red House when he was able to buy it was no longer what it had been.

Celia made coffee without interrupting the talkers. This time Iris accepted biscuits without comment. She seemed settled for the night, and by ten o'clock Celia was beginning to feel worried again. Could Iris possibly be expecting to be given a bed? Larry and Celia had two extra bedrooms, as Iris must know, but the rooms were almost empty. One was a dump for all the packing from their wedding presents and purchases, as well as for such things as pots of paint and bags of glass fibre. The other had a bed in it, with their spare blankets upon it, but no other furniture except a chair. Celia did not want to expose their poverty to an uninvited guest, who had no right to hospitality now she had recovered from her faint. Iris Anslow could not have come to the district with that in mind.

"Where are you staying, Mrs. Anslow?" Celia broke in, taking the bull by the horns.

"Nowhere," replied Iris promptly.

"Nowhere?" repeated Celia. "But you must have come from somewhere?"

"I was keeping house for an old gentleman. He died a week ago, and his daughter thought it was time I got out," said Iris. "I sent my trunk by rail, meaning to come to stay with an old friend. But I haven't written to warn her, and she never opens her door after nine o'clock at night. I'll have to find somewhere else."

"It's getting very late to look for rooms," said Celia. "But you can always go to a hotel. I don't want to hurry you, but don't you think you should be on your way back to town? Larry will see you to the bus, won't you, Larry?"

Larry hesitated. Celia thought she could read his mind. He was wondering whether they ought to ask Mrs. Anslow to stay. He was very soft-hearted, as Celia knew. She loved him for it, but felt that she was doing him a service in putting an end to his hesitation.

"You'll see Mrs. Anslow down the lane, won't you?" she repeated.

"Of course," Larry replied. He was still in two minds, she saw, rather like poor Bill Anslow. But he could not seriously want to keep this woman in the house for the night.

On the rare occasions when they had had a visitor—a girl from Celia's old office, a man who worked with Larry— Celia and Larry had walked her or him to the bus terminus. But Celia did not offer to go this evening, and Larry did not seem to expect it.

" You must come again some time," Celia said falsely, as Iris got to her feet. Iris replied with a brief,

" Thank you."

There was an odd look in her eyes, but Celia did not want to know what it meant.

SIX

CELIA WENT upstairs, switched the electric fire on, and began getting ready for bed. The evening had been a puzzling one. She was longing for the moment when Larry would get into bed beside her, and they would lie, with the bedside lamp still on, side by side, his arm beneath her, talking of the day's events, waiting to see how their mood would develop.

She undressed in a leisurely way. Larry seemed a long time. It occurred to her that she had never been left alone like this before. She had always known that Larry was downstairs, and about to come up. She was very conscious of the empty house. A strange noise worried her; it was some time before she traced it to a board which groaned as her foot left it.

Time passed, and then she heard the sound of the back door. She pulled her dressing-gown round her, and went to the head of the stairs.

"Larry?" she called into its narrow well.

He came through the living-room, and into the tiny hall, and stood looking up at her.

"I'll be with you in a moment. Get into bed," he answered. "I'm just locking up."

Celia returned to the bedroom. She heard Larry go back into the living-room. On impulse she put on her slippers again, and ran down the steep stairs to join him.

The living-room was empty. She walked through to the scullery. Larry was just shutting the pantry door. He turned as she came in, and leaned against it, looking the picture of guilt. She felt a laugh bubble up inside her.

"Are you hungry?" she asked delightedly.

"No," he said.

"Then what were you doing in the pantry?" she asked.

"The door was ajar. I was just shutting it," he answered.

"I could have sworn I had shut it," Celia said, vexed. "Don't tell me it has started opening itself? The draught from the window in there is awful."

She went to try the lock, but as she made to pass Larry he caught her in his arms. She gave to him, instantly, eagerly, and he held her, tightening his grip.

She kissed him, and he responded. Then he put her away from him.

"You're cold," he said accusingly. "You'll catch your

death. Run and get into bed. I'll be up in less than a minute."

Celia did as he told her. She hurried upstairs, and got into bed. The sheets were cold; in the agitation of the evening she had forgotten to put in a hot bottle. She rolled over on to Larry's side, getting it warm for him, listening to the sounds he was making downstairs, which she began to interpret so well.

The back door bolted. Through into the living-room. The front door bolts tested. Now up the stairs. They were really too steep to take quickly, but what a funny way Larry was mounting them tonight. Dragging his feet, as if he had four of them.

" Whatever are you doing?" she called, laughing.

Larry appeared in the doorway.

" Doing?" he asked.

His voice sounded guilty again, though Celia could not see his face. She wondered if he really had been going into the pantry to find something to eat, but had not liked to admit it.

" What on earth were you doing on the stairs?" she asked. " It sounded as if you were dragging the body up with you."

" My one slipper was falling off," Larry said. " I didn't want to stop and put it on properly."

" Lazy hound," she said affectionately.

He went into the bathroom. She could hear that he was having only a token wash. She could not blame him. It was cold in there. Heating everywhere; that was what they had to have next. But buying the house had cleared them out. Their margin was dangerously low; they must get a little money together again first. It was what they had

B

decided, after a short debate. Better together in poverty than a long wait, they had told each other. She suddenly wanted Larry beside her.

"What are you doing now?" she called. "What have you gone into the back bedroom for?"

"Just making sure that everything's O.K.," Larry said, and at last came and joined her, tilting the mattress as he climbed into bed.

He was cold, and his hair was wet. Laughing, tender, she set about warming him with her own body.

Celia felt awake, lively, and amorous, through her pleasure that Larry was back, and the incubus gone. But Larry, though affectionate, seemed abstracted. He had talked himself out, she supposed; and was remembering that he had to go to work in the morning. Disappointed, but acquiescent, she let him sleep, and presently fell asleep herself. But her mood coloured her dreams. At one time she dreamt that Larry was dragging Iris Anslow's limp body up the stairs, bumping on every step. While she was still filled with fear by the realisation that he must have killed her, she saw Iris's face, bathed in light, hovering in the darkness over her. The face was alive, to her unspeakable relief, but it was too near. She tried to strike out at it, but her arms were powerless. She woke, breathing fast, her heart pounding. Larry half roused, and put an arm round her in sleep, and she slept again, comforted.

In the morning Larry woke her, as usual, with a cup of tea. His doing this always made Celia feel guilty, but he was alert and cheerful from the moment he woke up, whereas she was drowsy and unco-operative for a full hour. This morning, like yesterday, she lay regretting that Larry should have to get his own breakfast, but doing nothing to alter the usual course of things. She turned her face up, eyes still half-closed, when he came to say he was ready to leave, and kissed him goodbye with all the fervour of her remorse. As soon as he had shut the bedroom door and gone whistling downstairs, by some perversity the cloud of sleep rolled away, and she wished even harder that she had had the courage to get up with him.

Celia made her own breakfast quite briskly, and by the time it was over was ready for the washing-up. As she did it, she planned her morning's work. The Red House had been very dirty, and, in the intervals of routine house-keeping for two, Celia was engaged in a room by room spring clean. The Belmont girls, too, she thought, ruefully, had been expected to be able to wash down walls, sandpaper and stain floors, paint, and paper, and de-rust; Iris had said so last night.

Celia went up to the second-best bedroom, prepared to put in an hour or two on its dirty paint. But on the landing she turned instead into the smaller back bedroom. It was an impulse; she remembered Larry going in from the bathroom last night, and how she had wondered what he was doing. Making sure that everything was all right, he had said. What was there to go wrong? Had he ever caught her leaving the window open all night? She did not think so, but, like a good housewife, she made a brief inspection.

All was as it should be, clean, quiet, and chill. She straightened the coverlet of the bed. Useful to be able to keep all their extra bedclothes on the spare bed, but they must be damp. If the weather turned icy there would be no question of simply picking up a blanket from here; it would need careful airing before use.

From airing Celia's thoughts went to the hot-water bottle

which she had failed to put into her bed last night. She might as well keep it by day in the spare bed, she decided; that would surely make a difference to the damp. She went into the bathroom to fetch and fill it. But it was not on its nail.

Celia liked to do a thing immediately she thought of it. She ran down to the kitchen. But the hot-water bottle was not there, either. Put off, she went back into the bigger bedroom, deciding to fill the bottle when she came across it. But its whereabouts worried her. She broke off to see whether she could possibly have made her bed the other morning with it still at the foot. It was not in her bed.

Mechanically, with a quite instinctive association of ideas, she went to look for it in the only other bed. She turned up the blankets, and it was there, at the very foot. Celia, although she had been looking for the bottle, could not have been more astounded at finding it where it was than if it had been the alarm clock, or egg-whisk. Astounded, she wondered whether she could, after all, have put it there herself, anticipating the idea which had occurred to her that morning; but she knew that she had not. Then Larry? Last night? It could only have been last night.

She took up the bottle. It was warm, with a ghost of warmth which evaporated as she tested it. So it must have been Larry, last night. But why?

The blankets were slightly wrinkled. Celia pulled them straight. Something caught her eye. She picked out a hair, a long, black, crinkled one, and knew at once that Iris Anslow had spent the night in this bed.

No one Celia knew well had naturally curly hair. Zelda Riddell had grey curls, which she kept short, in almost mannish style. But Celia did not trouble to make a list of acquaintances. She simply knew that Larry had brought Iris Anslow back last night.

She went through the sequence of his actions. His guilty pose by the pantry door. He must have shut Iris in as he heard Celia coming downstairs. The stairs went up over the end of the pantry; anyone within would know exactly when it was safe to come out . . . Then those extraordinary footsteps on the stairs, his drooping slipper. Larry and Iris Anslow must have been trying to tread as one, but, in spite of the staircarpet, the eccentric creaking of The Red House stairs had defeated them . . . Next the excursion from the bathroom into the spare room. Though Iris Anslow had slept in her clothes, the bed would be cold. Larry had seen the hot-water bottle, filled it, and taken it in. He ran no risk; he knew now how reluctant Celia was to leave her bed once she had got into it.

Had Iris Anslow left her bed, and come to look down on Larry and Celia in theirs, as in Celia's dream? Celia hated the idea, and came to the conclusion that there was no possibility of it. Apart from the lack of motive, there were the circumstances; Iris's head had been isolated in a ring of light, while the rest was darkness; all the characteristics of a dream.

But it was because of Iris's nearness that Larry had not liked either to talk or to make love, Celia realised with resentment.

Why had he brought Mrs. Anslow back? It was late, but not unduly so for travellers. She would have found the biggest hotel in the town open. Of course, she had not wanted to leave. Celia realised that now. That look had been panic. She had been frightened and resentful. But what did she expect?

No one was required to give hospitality for the night to a woman who had knocked on the door in error, or to an injured one, once she had recovered from her shock. And even if Iris had begged Larry to let her stay, what was he doing, agreeing to smuggle her in again without telling Celia? If there was some pressing reason—such as that Iris had found that she could not walk, and it was impossible to get a taxi, for instance—why on earth not explain when they got back?

Why, if it came to that, not shunt Mrs. Anslow on to her relations, at the corner cottage? But perhaps that would not do, since her Aunt Flora was living in sin there, though, to be sure, Iris had seemed remarkably tolerant of this.

Celia was forced to give up speculating. She was not even certain that she would be able to ask Larry frankly why he had done what he had. The fact was plain that he had not wanted Celia to know about it. It hurt and angered her, but she tried to occupy her mind with something else.

SEVEN

CELIA PUT in an hour on the bedroom walls, then left them to dry while she went to the shops.

At the corner cottage Bill Anslow was not in his garden, nor was the pseudo Mrs. Anslow peering out from behind her swathed nylon curtains. Celia wondered whether this was because the person they had been on the watch for had arrived, but dismissed the idea as fanciful. Nothing else had changed. At the grocer's and butcher's they still stared and made a silence as she entered, and at the cake shop she still had to queue, and then be served by someone who hardly deigned to glance at her.

When Celia got back to The Red House the first thing she did was to open the pantry door and peer in. It was a ridiculous thing to do, and she knew it. She pretended that she had meant all along to put her purchases away at once, instead of first taking off her coat.

The pantry was cold, and smelt of damp plaster. Celia kept glancing nervously at the far end, under the stairs, which was dim. Someone could have stood there, unobserved by anyone who merely opened the door and looked across to the window. But, of course, no one was there, and if Iris Anslow had hidden there last night her gritty shoes had left no trace.

Perhaps she had taken them off? She must have taken them off to come upstairs last night, thought Celia, and her flesh crawled at the idea of a stranger creeping up, and lying all night in the room across the landing, unknown to her. She wrested her thoughts away from Larry's treachery, and busied herself in the house.

Everything went well for the rest of the morning. In the afternoon Celia worked downstairs. She was troubled once by an extraordinary feeling that she was being watched through the windows, that when she lifted her head someone who had been looking in retreated just out of sight. There was a dark movement, just out of the range of clear vision.

It must be birds, on short low flights, in their fear that winter had already begun. Celia actually saw a bird, a black-bird, swooping low into a holly bush. But the sensation of being watched persisted, giving her a peculiar uncomfortable feeling which centred in the nape of the neck.

She made preparations for dinner, which they ate when Larry came in, just after six. Celia heard his footsteps as he came from the gate; they echoed as he went along the side of the living-room on his way to the back door. She rushed through the scullery to meet him.

They kissed.

" That smells good," he said, as he always did, this time referring to liver and bacon. Offal, shin, neck-of-lamb, sausages, Celia rang the changes on the dishes her cookery book said were inexpensive, not finding them as inexpensive as all that. But Larry had from the first been vociferously complimentary about her skill and her management, and it seemed as if his last few weeks' silence was over.

They ate as soon as Larry had washed his hands. After-wards they washed up together. Celia's nervousness had gone with his arrival. She planned to have a talk with him when they sat down again.

Before they settled by the fire Larry went out to the coalhouse, to bring in coal and wood ready for next day. He was gone some time, but he often found other odd jobs to do, so Celia did not worry. Then she heard him at the door.

" Celia! " he shouted.

Celia ran to the door.

" Give me a hand," he said.

But Celia, halting suddenly, let her hands fall, exclaiming, " Oh, not again! "

For it was Iris Anslow who was standing with him on their doorstep, her eyes half closed.

" Help me in with her," urged Larry.

" But where has she come from this time?" asked Celia rebelliously.

" I found her down by the old hen-houses; I think she may have been there all day," said Larry abstractedly.

No, she hasn't, thought Celia. Not this afternoon, anyway. She was wandering round, looking at me through windows.

" Shouldn't we take her to the doctor?" she said, still not moving to help, in fact, barring the way.

" If she feels ill," said Larry. " But I expect all that she needs is somewhere to rest."

He began to understand that Celia was reluctant to help. He moved past her, leading Iris to the fire. Celia stood where she was, and faced him when he returned to shut the door.

" Larry," she said, " have you thought? She must be mental. If we let her in tonight she may not want to go away again."

" We could give her a bed," said Larry.

" But there's no furniture! "

" She wouldn't mind," said Larry confidently.

" She didn't mind last night, you mean! " said Celia. She did not have to go on: Larry's guilty start was enough.

" But why?" she asked.

It was several questions she was asking him. Larry replied only to one.

" I was afraid you wouldn't sleep if you knew," he said.

" But why bring her back?"

" This is where she was born," he said.

Celia was astounded.

"But, Larry, we haven't any right to go back to where we were born! I once passed the house I was born in, in Leicester, and stared at everything, but I never expected the family there to let me stay," she protested.

"You were lucky. Some of us don't have a family," said Larry.

Celia stared. In all the time she had known Larry he had never put on a pathetic air about being an only child. Before she met him she had always understood that orphaned children were apt to take refuge in the pathos of their state whenever anything went wrong. Larry, on the contrary, had seemed rather proud of it, and fully compensated by the fact that his energetic mother regularly fostered needy children. Now here he was, asking for sympathy. Celia thought she knew why. He wanted Iris Anslow in the house. He had, as she always told her family, an extraordinarily nice nature, so he did not command or bluster. Instead, he was trying to make Celia feel sorry for Iris, because she was solitary like himself. Celia could have told him it wouldn't work.

"Why do you want her here?" she asked bluntly.

"She might be able to tell me something I need to know," Larry said shamefacedly.

"About someone who used to live in the lane?"

"Why do you say that?" Larry asked sharply.

He looked remarkably put out that Celia had stumbled on his reason. It seemed to her childish, but endearing, that he should have thought he was concealing the purpose of all those questions. When he acted childishly she loved him so much that it hurt. She reached up, kissed him, and docilely led the way back to the fire.

Iris Anslow was sitting by the hearth as if she belonged there.

She made no apology for her return, but, as soon as she saw that it was not to be questioned, relaxed, and settled back in her chair. Celia did not object, since that was apparently what Larry wanted, but she did ask where Iris had been all day.

Iris said she had spent the morning waiting in a doctor's surgery. He had seen her for two minutes, but said she was only bruised. In the afternoon she had been at the cottage.

" You went to your aunt?" asked Celia, in untactful surprise.

Aunt Flora had not made her very welcome, Iris explained without humour. They had had a row.

Celia imagined she knew why. She did not enquire about it.

" Shall you be sleeping there tonight?" she asked bluntly.

" No," said Mrs. Anslow.

It would hardly be decent, of course.

" We could give you a bed for one more night," said Larry.

Celia blessed him for that ' one more ', which told Iris that he had no secrets from Celia.

" I should be glad of it, if you're sure I'm not in the way," Iris said.

She spoke quite humbly, looking humbly at Celia, but Celia was irritated. Of course she would be in the way, what did she think!

" You won't be in the way," Larry said.

" I'm afraid you won't be comfortable," said Celia. " You

know our spare room isn't furnished yet." She spoke with meaning, but Iris showed no guilty reaction.

"We never had a spare room," she remarked. "When I lived here, if you asked anyone to stay for the night, it meant you had to share their bed."

"Tell us again about the old days here," said Larry.

EIGHT

IRIS SAID crossly that she hadn't particularly liked the old days. Larry, trying hard, replied that he had been sure that, with her good memory, she would have some very interesting stories about real old characters. Iris seemed to suspect him of making fun of her. To Celia's amusement, Larry was still not put off. He tried a different approach.

"There's a man at the pub in Littleworth who used to live in the lane," he said. "He never stops talking about what a dump the place was. According to him they were a lot of village idiots along here."

"What was his name?" asked Iris, rearing her head.

"Bailey. Victor, I think they call him."

"Victor Bailey! He never got nearer any of us than to beg for a lick of our lolly," Iris said scornfully. "The Baileys were no better than gipsies. When they came along everyone would rush to take in the washing, in case it got pinched. I wouldn't take his word for anything, if I were you."

" No, I thought that myself," agreed Larry.

He had done the trick. From the sins of the Baileys Iris proceeded to extol the virtues of the respectable families in the lane. But at least one example she gave was of doubtful value.

Thrift, for instance. The people in the lane were provident. But Iris's account of her grandfather's foresight was odd. In the Great War, rationing was not the well-organised thing that it had been in the Second World War. Mr. Belmont had had a whole sack of sugar, bought from a neighbour. This was illegal, Iris knew, though she was vague about the reason, since it happened before she was born. But she knew that the sack had been hidden under the floorboards in this very kitchen. She could show them the place, in the corner of the room behind Larry's chair. Ten to one, she said, that the trap was still only screwed down.

Larry was boyishly interested. Nothing would suit him but to look. They picked out the relevant floorboards easily, and with the aid of his tools he prised them up. The reward was a shocking smell of earth, damp and dusty at the same time, and a view of some broken pieces of brick. Iris Anslow came and peered in, then retreated with Celia away from the draught, back to the fire. It was one way of passing the evening, Celia thought, as she sat down again.

" However did your grandfather persuade a neighbour to part with a whole sack of sugar?" she asked idly.

" He worked at the Co-op," Iris explained.

" Your grandfather?"

" The neighbour."

" But even so . . ."

" He was satisfied. He did well out of it. He got a good half pig in exchange," said Iris. " My grandfather had a sweet tooth. It was agony to him not to have enough sugar for his tea."

" He kept pigs?" asked Larry.

It seemed to hurt Iris to admit it. But she did.

" Where?" asked Larry.

" Where?" Iris plainly thought he was daft. " In the pigsties," she said.

" Where are they?"

" Where they are now," she replied.

The conversation was distasteful to her. After every answer her mouth closed stubbornly.

" We haven't got any pigsties," said Larry.

" Of course you have. I thought old Yates would have pulled them down, but he hadn't got the energy, I suppose," said Iris.

" The agent called them henhouses," said Larry.

" They'll say anything. They don't know what they're looking at," said Iris, more animated in her scorn. " Of course, we kept hens in them, too. But they were built as pigsties. People used to say that it was a waste; that they were as well built as the house. My grandfather used to laugh, and be pleased. He was like that. Liked things good. Two brick-built sties, and concrete runs, with a good brick wall round and between them, and a loft over the lot, and a tiled roof. Sometimes people looking from the road thought it was a cottage."

" They're still rainproof," remarked Larry. " We haven't found a use for them yet, but I expect we shall."

" Pull them down," Iris advised.

Pull them down? It did not sound in character.

"Why?" asked Larry.

"More room for your garden. Use the bricks on the paths."

"A pity to pull down a sound building."

"It harbours rats," said Iris.

The idea of rats seemed to make her feel ill. Her face had grown white again.

Celia got up, and made a drink.

The conversation went back to the hole under the stairs. Larry thought it was a pity they had found no treasure in it. Mr. Belmont ought to have hidden something. Iris said that her grandfather had always told them that if they dug there they would come to Australia. When she was a child he had once put her down, and told her to begin digging, but she was alarmed, and cried to be let up . . . From that point they somehow came to talk about the loft; had they found anything up there? Iris asked.

Larry's architect had been up, but not Larry or Celia. There was nothing to go for, till they got round to insulating the roof. The tank was snug in the bathroom, the meagre electric wiring all ran under casing around the walls. The opening to the loft was by a hatch over the stairs, and only to be reached by sloping a ladder up from the landing. No one in his senses would have chosen to do this on an autumn evening, when there was a roaring fire to sit by, but Celia was not surprised when she found that she was helping Larry to rear a ladder up over the stair-well, and nudge the cover of the hatch along into the roof with the ladder's end. A bitter cold beat down, but neither Larry nor Iris seemed to notice it. Iris, who had so recently been half fainting, followed Larry up the ladder before Celia could do so. So

Celia was left to hold it steady, while the two of them prospected.

Larry was walking about in the roof—dull thuds indicated where he was. Iris was on the ladder—her head in the black hole, her body clamped to the ladder, her rather shapely thighs exposed to Celia's disapproving eyes. Iris's shoes were caked with mud, which confirmed Celia in her belief that she had been wandering round the garden. She was not entirely sane, in Celia's opinion, but since her inconvenient presence seemed to have brought Larry back from the abstracted silence in which he had lived for weeks, Celia was resigned to her.

Larry called down in a booming voice that there was a certain amount of junk in the roof, which would have to come out eventually, though it did not look the sort of stuff which would be a real danger in case of fire. An empty tin trunk, rusted till it was useless, and one or two oddments like picture frames, pushed up there out of the way. There were no documents proving that someone was the missing heir, no proceeds of a robbery stacked away, and not even a sack of sugar.

Celia laughed, and shouted back to him to come down before he got pneumonia, and the whole house was chilled. Iris, whose expression Celia could not see, began to crawl slowly backwards down the ladder. Celia helped her off the last rung, then sent her down to the fire, while she and Larry labouriously manoeuvred the hatch-cover into place from the landing, then took the ladder and put it back along the spare bedroom wall.

Everyone was rather dull after that. Very early they all went up to bed. Celia offered Iris a nightdress, and had it refused. She found sheets, and a towel, and filled the hot-water bottle. Then she and Larry retreated into their own room. The light went out; they lay clasped together, and whispered in the dark.

NINE

" How SHE can sleep in her slip! " said Celia in distaste. " I don't think she has had a wash, either."

" Warmer without one," suggested Larry.

" Will she want to stay all tomorrow? It doesn't sound as if she would be welcome at the cottage again."

" Try to keep her," begged Larry. " I don't think she'll want much urging, but try not to let her go till I get home again. I wish I could take a day off, but I suppose it wouldn't do."

" Take a day off?" exclaimed Celia. This was serious indeed.

" I'm afraid she only came back here because she's still in a panic. I wonder why? When she feels better, she'll be off again."

" But why does it matter? Why don't you ask her what you want to know?"

" Because she wouldn't tell me."

" How do you know? How do you know her so well?"

" Iris was one of the girls my mother fostered."

A weight rolled off Celia.

" Why didn't you tell me! " she exclaimed. " You mean you were brought up with her? So you still feel responsible for her? Like her brother?"

" I cetainly don't! " said Larry. After a pause, he went on, " I don't believe I think of her as a person now, at all. She's more like the lock I can't force or jiggle open, to get at what I want to know."

" What do you want to know?"

There was a short silence.

" I don't want to tell you," said Larry apologetically.

There was something in his tone which Celia found most touching.

" Then don't," she said reassuringly.

At that moment she was absolutely sincere.

" Tomorrow evening I'll work on her again," said Larry.

" I might, tomorrow, when we're just two women together, if you'll tell me what to ask."

" No, don't do that," said Larry quickly.

Celia was hurt.

" It's no use asking, with Iris," Larry explained. " She wouldn't part with information, once she realised someone wanted it badly, on principle. She wouldn't tell you her grandfather's age when he died, or what the weather was like yesterday."

" You do know her well! How long was she with you?"

" Ages. She wasn't official, of course. She ran away from the Belmonts to Mother. Mother persuaded them to let her stay with us till she wanted to go back. I don't suppose they minded, particularly. Anyhow, people aren't awkward with Mother. She knows what everyone should do, and tells them with such conviction that they do it. And even if it turns out badly in the end, they only think they must have made a mess of her instructions."

Larry spoke with humorous tolerance. The disagreement with his mother over buying The Red House did not seem to have harmed their relationship.

" Why did Iris run away?" asked Celia.

" Mother never discovered. Apparently she couldn't even guess. She wouldn't ask—said it wasn't fair."

" Why not fair?"

" She said, with rather touching naïveté, I thought, that it couldn't have been the fault of the Belmonts—they were much too respectable. By the way, one of the reasons she was annoyed with me for buying The Red House was that Iris had lived here, and Iris had become a problem. It was that which put her off, you'll be glad to know, not anything to do with the foundations."

" Poor Iris! " Celia said.

Larry sighed, and took his arm from around her.

" Time we were asleep," he said.

The next morning Celia struggled out of bed as soon as she sensed that Larry had left her side. Still asleep, not giving herself time to weaken, she pulled on her dressing-gown, trod into her slippers, and stumbled downstairs.

Larry was frying tomatoes and bacon. To her heavy eyes he seemed unnaturally alert and energetic. He was unflatteringly surprised to see her, and alarmed rather than pleased. When she had assured him that she was not feeling ill, he still did not ask for her assistance. He made coffee for her, and she drank it sitting at the table, trying to prop her eyes open, feeling as if she had been knocked on the head, while at frequent intervals Larry suggested that she should go back to bed again.

He would not even let Celia take up the cup of tea which he presently poured out for Iris. But Celia followed him, trailing behind. They found that Iris was out of bed, looking no more crumpled or unwashed than she had done last night, though she had slept in her underclothes, and not gone near the washbasin in the bathroom. She had smoothed out the coverlet of her bed, so that it looked almost hospital neat. The room showed no trace of her occupancy, but she had once more left the hot-water bottle under the blankets, as Celia noticed even in her drowsy state.

Celia asked if Iris had slept. Iris replied that she had. She seemed pale, but more lively than usual.

"Was this your room in the old days?" Larry asked.

"Aunt Flora and I slept here together, at one time," replied Iris.

"You would have a good view, before the new houses went up," said Larry. "I dare say you could see as far as the Anslows' cottage, couldn't you?"

"If you wanted to lean out and risk breaking your neck," said Iris. "You could see their washing on the line at the end of their garden, when the leaves were not on the trees."

"I suppose there was a great deal of coming and going from one house to the other," suggested Larry, standing propped against the doorway, as if his bus would wait all morning.

"Too much for Grandad," replied Iris with a sudden chuckle. "Aunt Flora and Mom and the other women used to make a gap in the fences and hedges so that they could slip through from one back door to the other. It made their husbands wild, to think of them gossiping like that when the men were away at work. But not even my grandfather could put a stop to it, though he did tell the Anslows they were not to cut across our garden to get next door."

" Did they do that?" asked Larry, in a shocked voice.

" Oh yes. We all did it. If anyone shouted after us we gave it up for a bit. But you can imagine we didn't fancy going out through the front gate, and down the lane, and up a drive again, when we could just walk through the hedge and across a back garden."

" I suppose the Anslow girls were always coming through the hedge to you and your mother," said Larry.

" There weren't any Anslow girls," replied Iris. " Only Bill and his brother."

" Oh," said Larry. His voice was blank. Celia looked at him, and his eyes were blank. She was suddenly very much afraid.

" You'll miss your bus," she said sharply.

TEN

AUTOMATICALLY LARRY turned and made for the stairs. He ran down, followed by Celia. In the tiny hall he grabbed her to him. She expected a kiss, but he whispered in her ear,

" Keep her here. Don't let her go. I'm afraid that she will go off again before I've got it out of her. Don't let her leave till I get back."

" I'll do my best," promised Celia.

She was offended, but Larry did not notice.

" Good girl," he said, and at last gave her a kiss, and snatched up his sandwiches and coat and was off. She heard him running down the drive. She rushed to the living-room window, to wave to him as he went up the lane to the bus terminus, but he did not look across at the house. Why should he? Usually Celia was in bed, and this morning he had other things to do than to remember that for once she had made the effort to see him off. Celia, knowing that she would feel for the next hour or so as if she had been dragged out of bed in the deepest of her sleep, thought bitterly that she need not have troubled to get up.

Iris came downstairs. She saw at a glance how Celia was feeling, and offered to get breakfast. Toast was all Celia wanted, and Iris set it before her, beautifully browned. Iris herself had a bacon sandwich. Afterwards she offered to pay for it, saying,

" I don't reckon it hurt you to give me a bed, but food costs money, and I can see that you're having a struggle."

" It's thoughtful of you," said Celia, " but Larry wouldn't want me to take it."

" Larry said you were welcome to stay with us for a day or two," she went on. " We have rather spent ourself out over the house, but it's not so bad as all that. And we understand that you can't go to your aunt . . ."

" It's very good of you," replied Iris. She sounded pleased, but not quite so grateful as Celia thought she ought to have been, seeing that they were complete strangers. Iris seemed not to have cured herself of thinking that she had some right to be in The Red House.

" It'll only be a day or so," Iris said. " I never meant to come back, but now I'm here I want to look around. Just for old times' sake," she added, " and to let Aunt Flora know that she can't have everything."

" How did she take your husband?" asked Celia bluntly. She was prepared to be snubbed, and to apologise. But Iris did not show offence.

" She didn't take him. I handed him back to her," she replied. " Bill was always soft about Aunt Flora. But my grandfather sent her off to train as a nurse, thinking she would be able to look after him in his old age. And then it turned out that the one who had to nurse him was me. It shows you; you can plan and plan, and work everything out as carefully as you like; it all comes to nothing in the end."

" Then how did you happen to marry Mr. Anslow?" asked Celia, determined to get the record straight.

" I told you," said Iris mildly. " Grandad wouldn't let Aunt Flora marry Bill; she was to be a nurse, and come back and look after him. Mother was delicate, after an operation she had. So, seeing that Aunt Flora couldn't have him, and that I was desperate to get married, I got Bill to marry me. It was no trouble. He had fancied Aunt Flora, but it was because he never dreamed he could have me. And I never dreamed he would, either, only . . ."

" Only?" prompted Celia.

" It was the lane," said Iris, suddenly passionate. " People were desperate to get away from it. People you'd thought would be always about went away, and didn't come back, or came back different, or died. So I married Bill. It didn't work out. He was always too soft for me. I never could stand a man who couldn't stick up for himself. If only just once he would dig in his toes, and tell you to take it or leave it! But Bill never would. Soft all through. So I left him. And his parents died. And some time after that, I'm not sure when, Aunt Flora moved in. She must have let on that she was married to him, for the people round here wouldn't stand her airs, otherwise. They never knew, not to say know, that Bill and I were married. I wasn't so proud of being Mrs. Bill Anslow that I boasted about it, and my grand-father had to be kept in ignorance; bedridden though he was, he would have raised Cain. He couldn't abide the Anslows, particularly Bill. He thought there was more to Keith, but he wouldn't have Keith around, either."

" What happened to Keith?" asked Celia.

" What happens to sailors?" said Iris Anslow angrily. " He was lost when his ship went down."

" Was he different from Bill?" asked Celia.

" As chalk from cheese," declared Iris.

She did not seem interested in Keith, but Celia liked to pursue a subject to its end.

" Not so soft?" she suggested.

" Keith was never soft at all," said Iris. " He had a gentle way with him that sometimes made you think that he was like Bill. Then suddenly you were brought up sharp. No, Keith wasn't soft."

" Did he have a girl?" asked Celia.

" You're very interested," said Iris suspiciously.

" Nosy," agreed Celia, nodding. " I'm sorry. It doesn't mean anything. I wonder about everybody. I've got Larry, you see."

" Larry's a nice chap," said Iris. " None of his mother's managing ways. Mind you, just occasionally I could see her in him. There's a set about his mouth. And his eyes. And to think that Aunt Zelda used to boast to Mom, when they were girls, that she could never have any children! She told Mom she'd had to have an operation when she was sixteen, and the surgeon almost wept. She used to tell everyone as a great secret, Mom said. Thought it made her interesting, I suppose. But she'd deny it if anyone reminded her, I dare say."

This was one subject which Celia did not wish to pursue to its end.

"Larry has nice eyes," she observed. "That was the first thing I noticed about him, I think."

"Keith had nice eyes, too," said Iris, in a quiet voice. "When he looked at you a certain way it was hard to remember that he was one of the Anslows, and the Anslows were no good . . . You were asking about a girl. Keith didn't have one, but if he had it would have been me."

ELEVEN

KEITH HAD no girl friend, thought Celia, her brain suddenly rousing from morning languor, in the way it had. So that would be why Iris ran away! It wouldn't be the first time that a girl imagined she was a boy's unattainable dream, and then found that he hadn't been spending his time sighing his heart out for her, after all. A sailor with caressing ways who had had no sweetheart! It wasn't possible.

Celia looked at Iris with examining eyes, and saw that she was in a mood to reveal sentimental secrets. But Larry didn't want Celia to question her. It brought Celia up short; that Larry should refuse her help. It made his attitude to Celia different from hers to him, and that made Celia slightly afraid.

She got up, and began to clear away the remains of their breakfast. Iris offered to wash up, and Celia allowed her to do so. It was one way of making sure that she stayed put for a time. Celia did not see how she would be able to keep Iris with her till Larry came back, if Iris changed her mind and decided to be off. So, as she dried the china, Celia rapidly reviewed in her mind the contents of her larder. It would not do to go out to the shops, and find on her return that the bird had flown.

There were eggs enough for an omelette. Celia could eke it out with diced vegetables. And in the evening they would have grilled ham and a really filling pudding, for Larry. Sponge with syrup, perhaps? Celia was not certain whether she had any syrup. She stepped into the pantry to make sure. While she was there she checked on flour, and went stooping to the far end, under the beginning of the stairs, to see whether any of the potatoes were not keeping. The chill of the pantry was not unpleasant. When she had had enough of it she came back to the kitchen end, put her hand on the doorknob as she stepped up, and found that the door would not move.

Celia gave a vexed exclamation, and put all her weight against the door. It would not budge. There was nothing for it but to ask Iris Anslow's help. She called softly, pushing as she did so, meaning not to make a very distressed noise in case the door suddenly gave, and let her stumble out into the kitchen, feeling a fool.

The door did not give. Celia called loudly, and banged on the wood with her fists. Then she stood back, and waited to be let out.

Iris did not answer, nor turn the doorknob. Celia had left her occupied in rinsing the dishcloth, after scrubbing the bowl. Perhaps she had stepped outside to peg dishcloth or teacloth upon the line? Celia called again, very loudly, and kicked at the door with her feet.

Nothing happened. Celia, not alarmed yet, wondered where Iris could be. Probably having a look whether Larry had dug any of the bulbs up. Celia listened intently, hoping to hear the sound of the back door as Iris returned to the house. She did hear a sound, and sighed with relief. Then she realised that it was not the back door which had just closed, but the door into the kitchen.

Iris had walked straight through the kitchen. She must be intending to sit by the living-room fire. Celia tried the door again, and found that, though the knob would turn, the door would not give. It seemed wedged tight at the bottom. She picked up the nearest weapon, her wooden bread board, and beat on the door with that.

It was a noise, she thought, to wake the dead. But when she left off, triumphant, silence was all that answered her.

There were several humiliating stages before Celia was forced to recognise that Iris was not going to release her. The woman must be mad. The woman was mad. Celia sank down dejectedly upon the step, tightened her cardigan round her chest against the cold, and waited, ready to begin banging again at the least sign of life from her guest.

If Iris sat by the fire it was not for long. When she moved again, Celia was up like a flash. If she had had a broom she could have rapped at Iris's feet, for Iris was going upstairs. Celia heard her walking level with her head, above her head, and then lost her on the landing. But there was no doubt about what Iris did next. She went into the empty bedroom, and dragged out the roof-ladder.

" She's going to look for me up in the roof! " exclaimed Celia, exasperated. " How can she be such a fool! "

She could not follow Iris's progress with the ladder, though when she thought of her, a frail-looking woman who had recently had concussion, holding a ladder out almost full length, and pushing with the unwieldly end of it at a hatch-cover in the ceiling over the stairs, she shuddered, and expected to hear the ladder crash down into the hall with a force which would split the old house open. But no such crash occurred; after a time there was silence.

Celia rested her aching arm. She turned to gaze at the frosted-glass window, but it was with melancholy regret. Larry had nailed it up for the winter, from the outside, because the draught had made the kitchen beyond untenable; there was still too much air from the air-brick above. There was nothing to be done with the window, short of smashing the glass. Celia tried the door again, and found it still immovable. She broke herself a crust of bread, buttered it by dragging it across the butter dish, and squatted down again on the step. If she was imprisoned, at least she did not need to starve.

An interminable time passed. Nothing happened. No one came to the house. The neighbours on either side all went out to work. Their contacts with Celia were limited to asking her to let the coalman in through the garage, or to warn the laundry man to pick up a bundle. They were not there, to wonder where she was, and arrive with the police to let her out.

Celia passed through the stages of irritation, resignation, and irritation again, and had started eating cake, when she heard sounds once more. She followed with her ears as Iris climbed down from the roof, shut the hatch, returned the ladder, and began to come slowly and heavily downstairs. She descended like someone who can hardly walk, and Celia did not wonder at it. Celia was ready for her as she reached the last stairs, banging from underneath like a demented blacksmith, at the risk of bringing the plaster down. Iris's feet halted for a moment, and Celia was triumphant as she heard her move on again into the living-room.

Iris's footsteps came out of the living-room; and went straight past. The back door opened, and then there was silence again. She had gone out of the house.

" She heard me! " exclaimed. Celia. " She must have heard me! She won't let me out. I shouldn't be surprised if it wasn't her who locked me in! " As she said this, she realised that it must be true. Iris had somehow wedged the door while Celia was at the far end of the pantry. Celia's eyes filled with tears of frustration and rage. It did not help her that she could now hear Iris opening the door of the toolhouse, just outside.

Another half hour went by. Celia had begun to believe that she would be here until Larry came home, unless she was willing to break the window. Then, when she had given up hope, the back door opened, and she could hear Iris turning on a tap.

Celia knocked again, in a fury. When she paused, worn

out, the pantry door jarred open, and Iris's voice said calmly,

" Is that where you are? I was wondering where you had got to."

Celia could not trust herself to answer. She rushed out, and turned to look at the door.

" The bottom was stuck," Iris said. " I had to work something out from under it. A piece of cement, I think it was."

She showed Celia some grey fragments upon the floor. Celia, in angry disbelieving silence, fetched the dustpan and swept them up. She threw them out of the open back door with one furious gesture, and after that her calm returned.

" Thank you," she said ironically. " I was beginning to think I was stuck in there till Larry came home."

" I looked for you," said Iris virtuously.

" Yes, I know," said Celia, containing herself. " I heard you."

" You weren't upstairs," Iris said, " so I looked in the garden."

" But you must have heard me banging? You're not deaf," said Celia. She could not keep the note of outrage out of her voice.

Iris chose to be offended.

" No, I'm not deaf," she replied haughtily.

" Well, you've let me out now," said Celia, with an effort repressing a thousand more things she could have said, deciding that she would be able to say them to Larry, and thus avoid bursting with indignation. " I'm going to have a cup of tea, to get over it."

She made tea, and they sat drinking on either side of the fire. But whether it was the angry knowledge in Celia's eye, or the return of her own inner disquiet, Iris had shed the matiness which she had developed over breakfast. She hardly answered Celia's remarks, and seemed restless as well as abstracted. When they had finished drinking, and Celia was removing the china to the sink, Iris followed her into the kitchen, and abruptly announced that she must go.

TWELVE

"WHERE TO?" asked Celia in surprise.

Iris showed that she thought the question unmannerly.

"It's time I went to my friend's," she said evasively.

"But you don't mean go for good?" demanded Celia in dismay. "Not this morning? Larry is expecting to see you when he gets back tonight."

Iris said that though she had not told her friend to expect her, her trunk might have been delivered by now, and the friend would be wondering why she didn't turn up.

"But can't you ring her from the village, and say you are here for another evening?" asked Celia. "She isn't expecting you at any definite time."

Iris said that she didn't see how she could do that. Pressed, she said that she hadn't anything to say to Larry; she wouldn't have thought he was interested now in how she was getting on. It was only three years ago since they last met, but it might as well be before the Flood, the way it seemed now.

"But Larry's not like that. He really loves to talk about when you knew him," protested Celia.

"Well, then he can talk to you about it," said Iris.

There was malice in her tone. Celia was reminded of the strange bold look she had given Larry that first night. She had to hold on to the knowledge that Iris was older than Larry, and that Larry had said he never thought of Iris as a person any more.

Iris continued unrelenting. But, in the end, Celia wrung from her the promise to return that evening for coffee and a chat. It was the best she could do. Iris went upstairs to get her coat. She had no luggage but her handbag. She could not even leave the place in a civilised manner, thought Celia. She announced that she would take a short cut through the back hedge. Behind the old pigsties it had always been possible to slip between an oak tree in the hedge and the hazel bush next to it, she said. She explained that in that way she could get on to the cart track in the field, which would bring her in a few hundred yards to the main road.

Celia did not hinder her. She supposed it must be a matter of not being seen from the front window of Bill Anslow's cottage.

In a marked way, Celia said "Till tonight then," instead of "Goodbye," and, feeling embarrassed by the idea of seeing a guest out through a hedge, remained by the kitchen door as Iris set off. Celia waved gaily when Iris reached the turn of the path round the wall which surrounded the pigsty run, but Iris did not look back. A moment later she was out of sight.

Celia went into the house. Her day was disrupted, but, without Larry, it always was a disorganised affair. She usually ate when she happened to finish a job, satisfying her appetite with anything which needed eating up. So she went back to work on cleaning the walls of the second bedroom. By a superhuman effort she had them all washed down by the time it was necessary to attend to supper. She and Larry would be able to paint the room as soon as the walls were dry again.

Larry was home promptly. He was carrying a box of chocolates.

" For you," he said in a low voice, as he handed them over; then, as Celia kissed him in gratitude, for their budget did not stretch to chocolates in mid-week, he added,

" I thought Iris might be suspicious if I brought her flowers. Now you can offer her a chocolate every time she stops talking; butter her up."

He grinned, inviting Celia to share the joke, without a suspicion, apparently, that he had wounded her.

Larry was displeased when she told him that Iris was not in the house. He agreed that Celia could not have detained her by force, if she really wished to go. But he seemed to think that she could have used charm, which again hurt Celia. And the evening was dominated by his expectation of Iris's return. Larry hurried over his supper, urged Celia to hurry over hers, and rose to help her wash up with unusual alacrity. From the moment they sat down afterwards he was speculating on what time Iris would arrive, and Celia feared at one time that he was going to leave her to sit alone while he met each bus.

It was fortunate that he did not do so, for Iris never came. At nine o'clock Larry began to realise that she would

C

not call, and that they had no address for her. Celia had never seen him so agitated. She told him that Iris must be settling into her new rooms, that she would come tomorrow, but he would not be reassured. At half past ten he decided to go to the Anslows' cottage and ask for her address.

" At this time of night?" said Celia. " They'll be in bed, surely."

" They're not so old as all that," said Larry.

Forty, fifty, sixty, Celia could rarely tell the difference. Anyone over thirty was a race apart. But she agreed that perhaps the Anslows were only between fifty and sixty, and that at half past ten they might not have gone to bed. But she still shrank from having Larry disturb them.

" They must be afraid of her. They didn't welcome her. She won't have told them where she was going to live," she objected.

" Of course she has. She's legally Bill's wife. And she's Flora's niece," said Larry. " Relations keep in touch, even when they disapprove."

Celia opened her mouth to say that they quite often didn't; the Anslows hadn't; then shut it again. She did not want to say anything to this new Larry which might indicate that she thought he did not know how ordinary families behaved. He might be touchy about that. She began to feel that the longer they lived together, the less well she understood him, and the idea distressed her.

Since Larry could not be stopped from going to the cottage, Celia agreed to go, too, though she was embarrassed at the idea of seeming to spy on a couple who were living in sin.

She got her coat, and followed Larry, who was already

champing by the back door. But as she passed the pantry Celia thought of something which might divert him.

" I wish you would look at the bottom of this door," she said, " I didn't tell you, but I was stuck in there for well over an hour this morning. The door had jammed, and I couldn't move it. If Iris hadn't let me out I should have had to try to break the window, or stay shut up all day till you came home."

It sounded pathetic; Larry was forced to pay attention.

" You must never try to get out of that window," he pronounced. " It's too small. But surely you could have forced the door?"

" Iris claimed it was wedged," said Celia. " By a piece of cement, she said."

" I don't see anything," Larry said, opening and shutting the door impatiently. " I'll have a good look in the morning. In the meantime, leave the door open any time you go in."

Outside, Celia made another bid to delay him. " This is the stuff," she said, producing some fragments from the yard.

" That's not cement, that's old plaster," said Larry. " And it wouldn't jam any door. It's rotten; with pressure it would simply crumble. But never mind it now. I'll have a look at the door tomorrow. Do come on. If you don't hurry, they really will have gone to bed."

He rushed off: and Celia had to follow.

The lane was livelier at this time of night than it had been all day, with cars being garaged at the new houses, doors opening and light streaming out, dogs being exercised. Just here and there the countryside lingered. A holly bush clipped like box, once part of a field hedge, still cast the pool of shadow in which rustic lovers used to embrace, though the hedge bank below was now crazy paved and covered with rock plants. The corner cottage garden had been trimmed off. The hedges which surrounded it were the wrong age, and the Victoria plum trees, once secluded, were within reach of any predatory hand. The front door, formerly a mere ornament, was now nearly on the pavement, and impatient tradesmen had brought it into daily use. Larry and Celia went up to it, and Larry knocked loudly.

There was a long interval. The sound of raucous music indicated that the telly was on. Larry found a bell, and rang it. Then they heard someone coming to the door.

THIRTEEN

IT WAS Bill Anslow who was holding the door open. He was full of apologies. They couldn't hear anyone at the door when the telly was on, he explained, but the bell fortunately interfered with the picture, so they knew when they were wanted, even though they couldn't hear.

He had got so far, when he realised who it was who was standing on his doorstep. His voice came to a stop, in a way which was very marked.

" Can we come in for a moment?" Larry asked eagerly.

Mr. Anslow stood aside. They could see his expression, which was embarrassed and reluctant. But, as Iris had said, he had no moral strength. They were unwelcome, but he would not say so, nor refuse to let them in. He showed them through the hall.

The narrow passage was almost filled by the coats hanging on one wall. He opened a door in the midst of them and ushered Celia and Larry into a small square sitting-room. This was the room which overlooked the bus stop, but tonight the curtains were drawn. The fire was blazing, the television set blaring and flickering. It was an oasis of comfort and consolation, a little warm bright box for two.

Flora Anslow was sitting with a black and white cat on her lap. She looked up as Larry and Celia entered, and then sat staring. Her husband said nothing, but moved another cat off a chair, and offered the chair to Celia. Then he looked round for somewhere to seat Larry. While the two men were both frenziedly pulling at chairs, and the noise precluded polite overtures, Celia and Flora Anslow had a good look at each other.

Flora was soft, too, Celia decided. She had a fair complexion, greying fair hair, and pale blue eyes. Iris Anslow had mobile features and bright eyes, but Flora plainly had always been muted. She gave the impression that she felt harried, and Celia could imagine her as a perpetual probationer, cap askew, hands fumbling, always a little behind, justly and unjustly castigated by Sister.

Bill Anslow got Larry seated. They all sat and looked at each other. In view of the Anslows' embarrassment and lack of social poise there seemed no need to lead up to anything. Larry said bluntly,

" We came to ask you if you had seen Iris."

The two looked at each other, simply for support, not for any concerted evasion.

" She was here yesterday afternoon," Flora said in a plaintive voice.

" Ah, that's right," Bill agreed.

" You haven't seen her this evening?" asked Larry.

" No, we haven't set eyes on her today," Flora said.

" Were you expecting her?" Larry asked.

" No." They were both hearty in denial.

" We were expecting her," Larry said. " She promised to call this evening, but she didn't turn up."

They had no comment to make; and their eyes did not seek each other's. Celia deduced that they knew nothing about Iris's plans; but Larry was harder to convince.

" Do you know where we can find her?" he asked.

They shook their heads.

" Surely she left you an address?"

" She hadn't got one," said Flora. " She said she had had to leave the place she worked in—the old man died. She hadn't got another job yet."

" But she had a friend she was intending to stay with for a bit," said Larry. " Surely she told you who it was?"

" No," said Flora.

" Didn't you gather where she was going to live?"

Flora shook her head.

" But you must know her friends! " Larry exclaimed.

" I don't think she has any, any more," said Flora. There was a touch of complacency; the rivals in love did not like each other.

" She had; she said so. Can you remember any names?" Larry said. " I want to get in touch with her, and she forgot to leave an address."

" I can't think of anyone," said Flora obstinately.

" And you?" Larry asked Bill.

" No. I can't call anyone to mind," he said instantly.

They were not trying very hard.

" Don't you help to support her?" asked Larry crudely.

Bill Anslow did not resent the question. He merely shook his head.

" Iris has always been able to look after herself," put in Flora, with spite.

Larry stood up, defeated.

" That may well be," he said in disgust, " but I don't think you realise that she was very far from well. She had been knocked down, and she seemed to be suffering from some kind of delayed shock. My wife was worried about her. We were expecting her to stay till she recovered. But she went out, and she hasn't come back, though she promised that she would. I think you should be worrying about her."

" There's nothing we can do," asserted Flora. " She'll let us know where she is when she thinks she will, and not before."

" Well, to me it seems very unsatisfactory, on both sides," Larry said.

He motioned to Celia to get ready to leave. Bill Anslow stood up to let them out. But as they were half way through the door Flora called after them,

" It won't be the first time that Iris has just walked out and not come back, you know."

Larry turned.

" Why? What do you mean?" he asked.

Flora had some colour now, and some indignant animation.

" She's done it before. Simply walked out, and gone off. Left the door open. Left my Mother and Dad helpless in bed, without a word of warning to them or to anyone. Now she's done it again, I suppose. It's no use your worrying. Iris is like that. You won't change her."

" Tell me about it," said Larry.

He stood over Flora, while Bill and Celia hovered, disapproving. But Flora did not need to be bullied or coaxed.

" It was when all the trouble was," she said. " My Dad had had a stroke, and Mother had her weak heart and her rheumatism. I wasn't allowed to come home and nurse them, because Iris was already there. It wasn't how they'd planned it—I was supposed to be the one at home. And I should have been glad. But it had to be Iris. Then, one day, Bill came and told me that Iris had gone off. Left them, both helpless or as good as, and the door wide open."

Larry waited for more, but Flora seemed to have done.

" It sounds like a brainstorm! " Celia said.

" If it was, she had her wits about her," Flora said, unconsciously sarcastic. " She remembered to take her clothes, and money. Money that wasn't hers to take."

" Now, Flora," said Bill warningly.

The intervention merely induced Flora to say more, more than she had meant to reveal.

" My father had a hundred gold sovereigns," she announced. " He used to keep them in a secret place. We knew, of course, but no one else. When I came to look, when I got home, they'd gone."

" Would that be what she was looking for in our house?" asked Celia involuntarily.

" No," answered Flora sharply. " She took them with her the first time she went."

Then she added suspiciously, "Looking for something in your house? Was Iris looking for something?"

"Under the floor, up in the roof, down by the pigsties," said Celia.

"Sounds as if she's really gone off her head," said Flora in surprise. "There was never anything in the roof, except some old junk that Mother wouldn't get rid of. Dad put it up there. We reckoned it wouldn't do Mr. Yates any harm, but we told him about it, just to be on the right side. We were pretty sure he wouldn't do anything about it, but it wasn't stuff that would burn. Under the floor was where Dad kept the sovereign bag. I suppose there's no harm in telling you now, but the hole was empty when Iris left home last time, as she has very good reason to know."

"Did she admit taking them?" asked Larry.

"As good as," said Flora.

"Did she?" Larry appealed to Bill.

"She wouldn't give a plain answer, but she as good as said she had," Bill answered.

"Did she explain to you why she went off like that?"

"No."

"We didn't ask her. We knew," said Flora triumphantly. "It was because her sailor boy came home after all."

Larry and Celia stared at her.

"Keith," Flora said, smiling at their stupidity. "Keith came home."

"She told me he had drowned!" Celia said.

"We thought he had. But he was picked up. He came home unexpectedly, months after everyone had given him up. Just sent a telegram, and came back from the dead. But by then Iris had taken Bill off me. Keith couldn't carry on with his brother's wife, could he? So Iris was trapped. And had her brainstorm, as you call it."

Flora was agitated, pink-cheeked, wild-eyed. Bill Anslow looked at her in slow dismay, then turned to Larry.

" I think you'd better go now," he said, with a certain dignity. " You see how it is. I don't think you need worry about Iris. She probably has her own reasons. She'll turn up again some time, if she wants to. And if she doesn't, we shall know she is all right. That's all you wanted, wasn't it, to know she was all right?"

" There was one thing more," said Larry slowly.

" Yes?" Bill was unsuspicious.

" Who is looking after the baby? Has she told you?"

FOURTEEN

" No. She wouldn't dare. Never," said Flora.

The black and white cat, startled by her vehemence, leaped from her lap, and began to stalk the floor, tail high, offended.

" We know nothing about a baby. Nothing has ever been said about anything like that, has there, Bill?" Flora went on angrily.

" No," he muttered.

" What are you asking for? Who sent you here?" Flora

continued. "It's Zelda Wright putting you up to it, I suppose? She always was a snooper. You tell her to mind her own business."

"My mother doesn't know yet that Iris came to see us," said Larry, putting the onus of the visiting where it belonged.

"Then I don't know what Iris has been saying, but it's nothing to do with Bill, whatever she said," Flora exclaimed.

"No. I'm sorry," said Larry. "We'll go. But you will let me know the moment you hear where Iris is, won't you?"

"We shan't hear where she is," declared Flora.

"But if you should."

"Oh, all right," she agreed crossly.

"Then I'm sorry to have bothered you. Goodnight."

Flora did not answer. When Celia and Larry walked out of the room she was irritably repulsing the cat, who had decided to forgive, and was trying to climb back to his evening home on her lap.

It seemed as if Bill Anslow might have made some remark at the front door. He cleared his throat, but thought better of speaking. Larry and Celia said goodnight, and went off along the path.

"You didn't tell me you thought she was searching the house," Larry remarked, as he took Celia's hand, and began to lead her back down the lane, towards The Red House.

"I didn't want to worry you," Celia answered.

"If the pantry door was as tight as you say, she used a wedge," said Larry. "Do you think she could put one in, while you were up the far end?"

"She was nippy enough with the roof ladder," said Celia. "It takes two of us, yet she did it alone."

"If she's searching for the sovereigns now, she didn't

pinch them all those years ago," pointed out Larry.

"Wonder if she's found them?" Celia said.

"If she hasn't, they're not in the house."

"Doesn't matter either way, then," Celia observed.

"No," Larry said, "except that I'd just as soon we hadn't had a thief sleeping with us."

"Yes," said Celia. She spoke blithely. If Larry had only known, her heart was not in it. At the first mention of a baby she had decided that she knew for whom the blue rabbit had been intended, and that Larry was keeping it at work because he did not know where Iris's child was to be found. What a fuss I've been making about nothing! she told herself, and brought her mind back to what Larry was saying.

"All those hints about Flora having taken something off her, and it not being Bill she meant!" she said tolerantly. "It sounds as if they each think the other has had the sovereigns."

"That's true. In that case, they may still be in the house."

"Unless old Mr. Yates found them, and latched on to them," said Celia.

"Nothing in it for us, either way," said Larry.

"No."

"How did you know Iris had had a baby?" Celia asked.

"She told me."

"But she won't tell you who looks after it? Did your mother ask you to find out, then?" It would have given Celia pleasure to learn that it was pressure from his overbearing mother that had caused Larry to take such a passionate interest in Iris's private affairs.

" Mother always says that she isn't interested in Iris any longer. But she would be glad to know, I think," said Larry.

" It sounds," Celia suggested, " as if Iris might be a little mad."

" As Flora said, if she was mad, she had her wits about her," answered Larry. " But never mind, retribution is at hand."

" What do you mean?" asked Celia.

" Oh, how do I know? Forget it," Larry answered, and pulled her into a run. He raced her up the drive to the house.

They waited for Iris next evening and every evening, but she did not come. For a week Celia hardly dared to walk down to the shops, in case she missed her. At first Larry seemed confident that she would turn up; afterwards, when they began painting the bedrooms, he ceased to refer to her. But Celia believed that he was thinking about her. Once he let out that he had discussed with a man at work the ways of tracing someone who was missing of her own free will. Afterwards Celia said to him,

" You're not really thinking of trying to find her, are you?"

" Why not?" asked Larry, answering her tone.

" Well," Celia said, exasperated, " what good will it do you?"

" None at all," Larry returned crisply.

Faced by such definiteness, Celia was silent.

The dingy walls of the bedrooms of The Red House became gradually clothed in bright paints, petunia, and primrose, and lilac, as odd in that setting as Chinese papers, but much more cheerful. And the sun flooded into the high-ceilinged rooms, because the winter was mild. But, as Celia hoovered, her singing was apt to stop suddenly without her realising it, as she listened for a footfall that never came, or her nerves were thrummed by the finger of a premonition which would not be ignored. The question of the anonymous letter, of the blue rabbit, had lost all urgency—that was something gained—but they had become part of a general and vaguer uneasiness.

FIFTEEN

CELIA WAS alone when the private detective came. He expressed surprise that her husband was not at home, and said that he would call again, later, but Celia thought that he ought to have known that Larry would not be back from town by five o'clock. The man had turned up just late enough to make it feasible that some husbands would be back home, just early enough to ensure that this particular husband would not be, she worked it out afterwards. At the time she took his words at face value, and invited him in to wait. He was a youngish man, in a raincoat, with a long face and tired eyes. His name was Burbage.

Celia stood irresolutely in the kitchen, because he had not followed her movement towards the living-room.

"What did you want to see my husband about?" she asked.

"Some enquiries I have been asked to make," he replied vaguely.

"Can I help you?" Celia asked.

"Perhaps," he agreed.

"We'd better go through into the sitting-room," Celia suggested. This time, after a frankly curious look round the kitchen, he consented to follow her.

The table was already laid for supper. Celia cast a glance over it, and felt she need not blush for her housekeeping. And then she remembered the bowl.

Larry's mother had bought them a fruit bowl at a sale. It was of china in a pretty blue, but had a curious flat shape which was not very useful. Larry said that it was meant for a dog, and always referred to it as 'the dog's bowl'. Today, feeling skittish, because she had bought chicken, and Larry was expecting mince, Celia had placed the blue bowl in the centre of the table, and arranged upon it two dogs' rubber bones, skimpily but coquettishly garnished with parsely. Larry would laugh, and Celia unconsciously counted his laughs nowadays, and stored them in her mind as proof that all was well.

She now cursed the longing for Larry to be back that made her have everything ready for him hours too soon. There had been absolutely no need to lay the cloth. And this man was staring at the bones, his face deliberately expressionless. If he had looked less solemn, Celia would have explained airily that it was just a joke. But she could imagine in advance his wooden unbelieving assent, and her courage completely failed her. Perhaps he would imagine she and Larry were the sort of besotted couple who sat their dog on a chair to eat his dinner at the table with them? That would not be so bad. But, against that, there was no sign of a dog in the house.

Celia gave up. Let him think what he liked. She saw his glance leave the bowl, and his face settle into a non-committal look from which she gathered that he thought she must be mad. She resolved to make her answers to his questions very calm and businesslike.

" I understand you and your husband are friends of Mrs. Iris Anslow," he began.

" Has something happened to her?" asked Celia, in such panic that she was obviously neither calm not business-like.

" Have you reason to suppose that something might?" Burbage returned.

" No. No, of course not," protested Celia.

" But you seemed to be expecting it?"

" Well, it's what everyone would think, isn't it, if people come making enquiries?" said Celia.

He seemed to accept that.

" What has happened? What is the trouble?" Celia went on.

" Probably nothing. She seems to be missing. Her land-lady is alarmed."

" Oh, but she's done it before," put in Celia.

" Done it before?"

" Just disappeared, without a word to anyone."

" You've known her a long time, then?"

" No. Oh, no. I'd never heard of her until a few weeks ago."

" That was what I understood," he replied, and left Celia to realise that he saw a discrepancy between that statement and her knowledge of Iris Anslow's past history. Celia was rendered ill at ease, though her conscience on the point was clear.

"Her Aunt Flora told us that Mrs. Anslow had gone off before, when she lived in this house," she explained. "She just left the door open, and her grandparents ill in bed, and walked out, without a word to anyone."

"It's the aunt you know well?"

"Oh, no. I've only seen her once, for a few minutes, three weeks ago."

Burbage's silence seemed to underline the oddity of being so much in Flora Anslow's confidence, if what Celia said was true. Celia was beginning to be afraid to say anything, so this time she did not elucidate.

"I understand Mrs. Anslow was staying with you here, in this house, three weeks ago," Burbage said, taking out a notebook, and studying it.

"Well, not staying, exactly," said Celia. "We put her up for the night."

"Only one night?" Burbage asked.

"Yes," said Celia. Then she hesitated. It had been two nights, of course.

"You were going to say?" Burbage prompted her.

"Nothing. She collapsed on our doorstep, and we gave her a bed."

"Just for a night?"

"Two, actually," said Celia airily.

Burbage passed the correction.

"You didn't know her before that?"

"No, not at all. But my husband knew her when they were younger. He'll tell you."

"I'll ask him. What was the matter with Mrs. Anslow?"

"She had been in an accident."

" What did the doctor say? You got a doctor, of course."

" No, we didn't get a doctor."

" You found her collapsed on your doorstep. You took her in, but didn't send for a doctor?"

It sounded about as mad as rubber bones on the table for supper.

" She went to one next day. She only came here by mistake," said Celia defensively.

" When she left you, did she give you any idea where she was going?"

" To a friend, she said, who was expecting her."

" The name and address of the friend?"

" She didn't tell us that."

" She left without saying where she was going, and without giving you any address at which she could be found?"

" Yes."

" But you had taken her in when she was ill. It would have been natural for her to tell you, to allay your anxiety about her."

" Well, she didn't."

" Did she refuse, or did you not ask?"

" I didn't ask. She promised to come back that evening."

" You were expecting her back?"

" Yes. I had asked her to come back for a chat when my husband was home."

" What was the chat to be about?"

" Just a chat," said Celia.

" Did she come?"

" No. We waited for her till half past ten, and then we went round to the Anslows, at the top of the lane, to ask if they knew anything about her."

" Why did you do that?"

" We were anxious to know why she hadn't turned up."

" Could they tell you anything?"

" No, except that she had done that sort of thing before."

" So you gave her up. Did you do anything more about her?"

Had Larry?

" No," said Celia defiantly. " We forgot her. She was nothing to do with us."

" You were simply Good Samaritans, in fact?"

He made it sound a rather dubious thing to be.

" Yes, that was it," said Celia.

" Well, if you don't mind, Mrs. Riddell, I'd like to come back when your husband is at home, just to make sure I have the dates right, and the details."

" Of course," said Celia. " Larry shouldn't be very long. Will you sit down?"

" No, thank you. If you'll tell me what time you have supper, I'll come back afterwards. Let your husband have his meal. He'll find his memory working more easily, I expect, when he's been fed."

His glance travelled to the dog's bones; then he consciously averted it.

" That's just a decoration," protested Celia.

" I didn't think you were going to eat them! " Burbage said.

He probably imagines Larry and I have had a row over my cooking, and that this is how I welcome him when he comes home tired from work, thought Celia.

" It's a joke. I thought it would amuse my husband. He likes my cooking, actually," she said.

It was surely Burbage's cue to say " I'm sure he does," but he looked astonished.

" Well, about seven, then," he said, and turned to go out of the room.

SIXTEEN

CELIA SAW Burbage out, and closed the back door behind him. Her anxiety subsided. By seven she and Larry would have had their meal in comfort; then Larry would enjoy a talk with another man. Celia went to the table, however, and removed the dog's dish. Jokes were not appropriate when someone one knew was reported missing, had perhaps come to harm.

Celia made the mistake of wondering what harm Iris Anslow could have come to.

When adults disappeared, persons who had the right to be interested first made enquiries as best they could, just as she and Larry had gone to Bill and Flora Anslow, to see if those two knew anything. It was only when all else failed that one hired a detective. Had the detective said that the landlady was alarmed? Was it merely that she wanted her money? But no, Burbage had definitely said that the landlady was alarmed. Well, Celia would have been so, too, if she had been a friend, for the accident seemed to have affected Iris Anslow's mind. Her behaviour at The Red House had not been normal.

Would Celia have to tell Burbage how Iris had shut her up while she searched the house? And what it was they believed she had been searching for? Celia would not object to telling about it, for it made a good story, and one that would satisfy any stranger, that Iris Anslow had schemed to get into her old home to search for a hoard of gold sovereigns. That was normal, conceivable. But all the rest, about Larry's insistence on trying to help her—how careful they would have to be not to be drawn into any reference to that.

Anyone at all would find Iris's subsequent disappearance embarrassing, Celia thought. But she and Larry could not give any help. Larry had been passionately interested in Iris's movements while she was around, but, when she went away, after that one effort to find her, he had accepted the situation.

Or had he? He had certainly ceased to speak to Celia of it. Since the first two or three evenings after Iris failed to turn up he had not referred to her again. He had seemed once more absorbed by his work, and the redecoration of the house. And was such a change normal?

Celia thrust the idea aside. If Larry had seemed frantic one minute to find Iris, and supremely indifferent the next, that could be explained in a variety of ways. There was absolutely no justification for her sudden fear that he had not, after all, accepted the situation, that he had, unknown to Celia, gone searching for his foster-sister again. He had the dinner hour, when he said he played cards or went shopping, after eating his sandwiches—(the canteen food was poor, and dirty, as well as expensive.) If he gobbled his snack he could get three-quarters of an hour every day in the centre of town, to watch the passers-by, or play detective.

And had he done so? If he had come across Iris again, would it mean anything? Larry wouldn't cause her to disappear. Larry wouldn't hurt a fly.

Iris Anslow is not a fly, thought Celia. She is a woman from whom Larry very badly wanted information. About something he could not and would not explain, information which Iris deliberately would not give him. Iris was behaving badly to Larry; remembering that, would Larry treat her badly? Celia thrust the thought aside.

Iris had left The Red House a satisfied woman, never intending to come back. Celia was aware of that now. If it was sovereigns Iris had been searching for, then she had found them, or found out what she wanted to know about them. She had been almost smug, as she went away, and quite uninterested in pursuing the acquaintanceship with Celia, or in a gossippy evening with Larry. She would never have come back. And she had been definite about where she was going. A friend was expecting her, would worry if she didn't turn up. She had every intention of not allowing the friend to worry. She would not have alarmed her by disappearing without a word. Unless she couldn't help it.

At that point Celia thrust the problem aside again, and went to look at her chicken. She had the casserole ready to put on the table long before Larry's step was heard on the drive.

For once Celia had startling news to tell, when he asked her what sort of day she had had. And she wished passionately that she could have been reciting her old rigmarole about the people who had stared at her when she went shopping. (She knew now that the locals were interested in The Red House for old times' sake, and marvelled to see a young couple like herself and Larry in the place of the patriarchal Mr. Belmont, and the age-old Mr. Yates.)

" A private detective is coming to see you tonight. About Iris Anslow. They don't know where she is. Her landlady is trying to find her. The man's name is Burbage, and he will be here at seven," she reported.

She came out with her news all at once, in throw-away style, so that she should not seem to attach any special importance to it, but she watched Larry's face like a hawk.

He was startled; there was no doubt about it. How she wished now that he had a less readable face!

" A detective?" Larry exclaimed. " They don't make enquiries about people who go missing unless there's something fishy, surely?"

" I expect she owes the landlady money," said Celia.

" Could be that, I suppose," said Larry. But he brooded. He did not come to life again, in spite of the chicken, till Burbage arrived.

Burbage greeted Celia this time like an old friend. Larry got on with him at once, like an old friend. Larry liked people. Celia could have wished, this once, that he did not. With his eager interest, his willingness to talk, he was putting himself in danger, if he had anything to conceal.

They began with the courtesies. It turned out that Larry and Burbage had attended the same school. Larry said that he had never seen Burbage since. Burbage admitted that he had not remembered Larry, or known that he lived in The Red House, though for some years he had been in the local police. Larry said that he supposed that most of the people in the lane were quite unknown to the police. Until they were burgled, or had their cars stolen, or locked themselves out.

Burbage admitted with some reluctance that the lane, in his time, was not a den of crime.

" Everyone around here is extremely law-abiding," Celia said, anxious to have the point admitted.

" Oh, I don't know about that. It's only a question of degree, after all," said Larry. " I was thinking the other day, looking at all these new villas, that they've probably got their secrets, just like The Red House. The unlicensed television, the income not declared, the reference forged, the hose used in a drought, the child ill-treated. I bet there isn't a house in the lane which hasn't got something on its conscience."

" We're not as bad as that," protested Celia.

" May one ask what The Red House secret is?" asked Burbage with a smile.

" If these walls could speak!" said Larry, gazing affectedly round the room.

" Mrs. Riddell wouldn't care for that," said Burbage. " She looks quite alarmed."

He was right. Celia had been on the point of grabbing Larry's arm to warn him to be careful what he was saying; she felt that they could not afford to spark off enquiries into the secrets of The Red House.

" I don't think it's right to be funny, if Iris Anslow is really missing," she said primly.

" Very proper," said Burbage sceptically. " Suppose we get down to business?"

SEVENTEEN

He took Larry quickly through the history of Iris's appearance at The Red House.

Larry volunteered, what Celia had suppressed, that they believed Iris had searched the house.

Burbage seemed in two minds. On the one hand, nothing in human behaviour was too curious to believe; on the other hand, the theories of the inexpert were not to be examined seriously. He took it for granted that Larry's idea was to demand the return of the sovereigns, if they existed; whereas, in fact, Larry and Celia had not realised that they might have a claim on something so obviously not their property. However, on balance, Burbage seemed inclined to doubt whether the sovereigns had ever existed, and he was more sceptical still over whether, if they did exist, Iris Anslow could have found them, and taken them out of the house.

Had Celia ever had a sovereign in her hand? he asked.

Celia had not; but she would not have admitted to it, if she had. She thought Burbage naïve to suppose she would. But he was merely making a point. A bag containing a hundred sovereigns would be heavy, he explained. He could not say, off-hand, how heavy, but it was not something one could put in the pocket.

Larry reminded him that Iris had gone from upstairs out into the garden; she had had ample opportunity to leave the bag of gold where she could pick it up later.

And good reason to look smug, and guilty reason not to return as she had promised, Celia exclaimed enthusiastically, seeing Iris Anslow slipping happily with a bag of gold towards the bus-stop, and out of their lives.

" Is that your theory?" asked Burbage, staring at her. " That's your considered opinion of what has happened? That she found her grandfather's hoard, and has made off with it? And so doesn't want to be found?"

Celia shrank back a little. " I haven't any theory, really," she declared uneasily.

" I always thought," observed Larry, coming to her aid, " That the police took no steps to trace missing persons unless they had reason to believe that harm had come to them. Or that they had done something criminal. Why is the landlady different? Does Iris owe her money?"

" No one has suggested that Mrs. Anslow has done anything criminal. Not until you spoke of the possibility," said Burbage.

" She doesn't owe her landlady money?"

" The landlady doesn't admit to being a landlady. She isn't supposed to let. She says that Mrs. Anslow stayed with her on a friendly basis, and sent her flowers, or such like, when she left."

" Then what are you doing here?" demanded Larry. " You surely wouldn't take the case on if someone simply left without saying goodbye, or sending flowers. What is it? Has Iris gone off in her nightie without putting her plate in?"

" Did she have dentures?" asked Burbage keenly, taking

out his book. " Mrs. Pole—the landlady—didn't know."

Larry hesitated. " Did she?" He appealed to Celia.

Celia considered for a moment, summoning up Iris's face.

" Yes," she said finally. " Yes, I'm sure she had. " She had that flat look under the nose. It spoilt her face. She could have been very striking."

She looked at Larry, hoping he would contradict her. He returned her look without understanding.

" Did she go off without her clothes?" Larry asked Burbage.

" No. That is to say, there were no clothes that shouldn't be there left behind in her room."

" Then what makes you suggest that she has been a victim of foul play?"

" I don't think I have, have I?" said Burbage.

He enjoyed the astonishment he caused.

" I don't mind telling you the facts," he said handsomely. " I think you'd better hear what has happened, in case, on reflection, you can throw any more light. Mrs. Pole, the landlady, reported to the police that Mrs. Anslow had disappeared. Gone out, probably just after lunch, in her hat and coat, but leaving everything else behind her. And there has been no word since."

" But that's not serious," exclaimed Larry. " People often do that, we're told. For reasons that seem good to them."

" Yes, that's quite correct."

" But why try to make it into something sinister?"

" Because on the day, and about at the time, that Mrs. Anslow seems to have disappeared, the landlady claims, and her doctor supports her, that someone attempted to strangle her."

" Tried to strangle Iris! " exclaimed Celia.

No one would ever know into what dark pit she looked at that moment.

" Not Mrs. Anslow! " said Burbage rebukingly. " Mrs. Pole."

Celia's breathing steadied.

" Someone tried to strangle Mrs. Pole? " she asked wonderingly. " What for? Who?"

" Questions we have to ask ourselves," said Burbage briskly. " It seems established that there was an assault, and that it coincided with Mrs. Anslow's disappearance. Was it Mrs. Anslow who committed the assault, and then left? Or was Mrs. Anslow also attacked, and somehow disposed of? You can see that the police are interested in finding her."

" Surely Mrs. Pole can tell you whether it was Mrs. Anslow who tried to strangle her? " said Larry. " It's not a thing which can be done from the next room, surely?"

" The next room? " said Burbage.

" I mean, from a distance," said Larry. " If Mrs. Anslow was actually in the room strangling her, surely Mrs. Pole must know. Or has her memory gone?"

" She's not a young woman," said Burbage. " But she has stood up to the shock surprisingly well. Tough as an old boot. But, as regards your question about strangling someone without being seen, of course it can be done. From behind."

" Oh," said Celia, shuddering.

" Mrs. Pole," said Burbage, turning to her, suddenly loquacious, " lives in a small terrace house in town. You may know the type. Front door opens into the front room; you go along a passage, past the cupboard under the stairs, and you're in the kitchen living-room. The scullery is beyond, with the back door. Stairs off the kitchen. Mrs. Pole allowed Mrs. Anslow the front rooms, up and down. It was not at all convenient, because to get upstairs Mrs. Anslow had to come through the kitchen, which was Mrs. Pole's sitting-room. Likewise if Mrs. Anslow wanted to cook in the scullery. But Mrs. Anslow had stayed with Mrs. Pole before, for holidays, and she was considerate. Mrs. Pole had no complaint.

The two women usually had an early lunch together. Mrs. Anslow helped wash up, and they made and drank a cup of tea. Then, while Mrs. Pole had her afternoon nap on the sofa in the kitchen, Mrs. Anslow went back into her own room—the next room, as you said, Mr. Riddell."

He paused.

" Yes," said Larry.

" On this particular day, exactly three weeks ago," said Burbage, looking disappointed, " they kept to their routine. It would be about a quarter to one when they parted, and Mrs. Anslow didn't say what she was going to do, though she sometimes walked in the park, or simply sat and read in the front room. Mrs. Pole can't say whether she went out or not, or when. But some time during this afternoon nap of Mrs. Pole's, Mrs Anslow disappeared. And someone came through, from her front room next door, and tried to strangle Mrs. Pole with the stocking which she always bound round her eyes, to keep the light out, so that she could get off to sleep easily."

" You know that he came in through the front room?" asked Larry.

" The back door was still locked and bolted when Mrs. Pole was able to get up and investigate. She hadn't the

strength to undo it. The front door was open. She went
through it to ask the people next door to ring up her
doctor."

" She wasn't badly hurt, then," said Celia. She was
relieved that she could safely express the joy that had filled
her from the moment she heard it was the unknown Mrs.
Pole who had been attacked.

" No, she had a certain amount of bruising, in spite of
the stocking, pain in the neck and jaw, and so on. She
didn't put up any struggle; she thought at first that she
was dreaming. But the stranger gave over just when she was
sure that she would suffocate. She fainted, and lay like
that for a time; then she got up, and went for help."

" It must have been a terrible shock," said Celia, her
cheerfulness breaking through.

" Yes, and the question arises; why wasn't the job done
properly? Did the stranger think he had killed her? Was
he so incompetent? Did he perhaps repent midway? Or did
he bend down, as he was about to finish her off with his
hands, and see that he had got the wrong woman?

" Oh, no! " said Celia.

The black pit loomed beneath her feet again. She dared
not look at Larry for support.

" No?" said Burbage. " But it could be, don't you think?
Of course, the police haven't heard anything about a hundred sovereigns. More like two thousand pounds wouldn't
that be, now? and murder has been done for shillings. Mrs.
Pole is a widow, and old-age pensioner, whose life has
always been an open book. Mrs. Anslow, on your showing,
is something of a mystery. Why shouldn't it be Mrs. Anslow
the stranger was after, unless the stranger was Mrs. Anslow
herself, which isn't the easiest thing to imagine."

EIGHTEEN

" No ONE would want to strangle Mrs. Anslow," said Celia, as firmly as she could.

" If he mistook one woman for the other he couldn't have known much about either, of them, surely?" said Larry. " You said just now that their habits were very regular."

" He could have been a stranger. In fact," said Burbage, " there is some evidence that a stranger was enquiring after Mrs. Anslow the day before the attack."

" Well, then," said Celia, with relief.

Burbage looked at her curiously, and she bit her lip.

" The next door neighbour told us that someone came enquiring for Mrs. Anslow the day before," Burbage went on. " During the lunch-hour, about the same time as the attack next day." •

Celia could not for the life of her avoid making a sound of dismay.

" Yes?" said Burbage.

" Nothing," she answered. " Go on. I was listening."

" The neighbour didn't pay much attention to the caller, unfortunately," said Burbage. " She was annoyed at being disturbed at her dinnertime. She apparently opened the front door the merest crack, and listened to him round it, then indicated that he had the wrong house. But she gave me a description, of a sort."

" What did she say ?" asked Larry.

" She said he was young. About your age, I gather," said Burbage. " He was wearing a fawn raincoat. No hat. He had thick dark hair."

He paused for a moment. Celia thought that he had glanced at Larry's thick dark hair as he spoke.

" She said he had a round face, and a good colour," went on Burbage. This time his eyes definitely lingered on Larry's face, with its eager round contours, its healthy red and brown.

" He was not very tall," continued Burbage, fixing Larry immovably now. " But what she remembered most distinctly was his voice. Very pleasant, she said it was, young and quick. A slight local accent. What struck her most, though, was that he had a bit of a hesitation. Not quite a stammer, nor a lisp, but a sort of hesitation over the s of Anslow. It stayed in her mind when she had forgotten what he looked like."

Larry only stammered when he was agitated. Celia prayed that he would not stammer now.

" She seems to have noticed a great deal," Larry said with a rueful grin.

" Well, it often comes back to people, if you make them take it slowly," said Burbage complacently. " Was he tall or short?' ' Oh, I don't know at all!' ' Well, was he as tall as I am?' ' Oh, no, only about up to your shoulders.' You know the sort of thing."

" I see," said Larry.

" Yes. Well, now, would you care to tell me what you were doing around there that day?"

" Don't! " exclaimed Celia involuntarily.

Burbage looked at her in surprise. Larry deliberately did not glance her way.

" You do agree that you were the man? " said Burbage.

" Yes, of course," said Larry. " There's no mystery about it."

" But you don't seem to have told your wife," said Burbage.

" I didn't want to worry her," declared Larry. " It wasn't as if I'd managed to see Iris, after all."

" It would have worried her to think that you hadn't been able to see Mrs. Anslow? " said Burbage sceptically.

" She was worried about the whole business. She didn't want me to have anything to do with Iris."

" I see," said Burbage; seeing all sort of things.

" I went round in my dinner-hour," said Larry. " I had phoned my mother the day before and asked her if she knew any of Mrs. Anslow's friends in town. She suggested Mrs. Pole. She didn't know her address, but had an idea it was one of the houses in Eastfold Street. So I went there."

" Yes," said Burbage.

" I tried the wrong house first," said Larry. " The woman next door was cagey; but she admitted that Mrs. Pole had a lady staying with her. She said they had a rest about that time, wouldn't thank me for disturbing them. So I banged the front knocker rather gently. Nobody came. Then I went up the entry and round the back. The kitchen curtain was one of those half way things. I looked over the top and could vaguely see someone lying on a sofa. So I didn't knock again. I went away."

" Mrs. Pole did hear you knock, and see you look in, but

D

she didn't get up," Burbage said. " Mrs. Anslow was up-stairs, getting ready to go out. When Mrs. Pole told her about the caller, she suggested at once that it would be you. She said it didn't matter: you would be sure to call again, next day."

" I didn't," said Larry quickly. " I didn't go back at all."

Burbage was incredulous. He did not trouble to hide his unbelief.

" You went to the trouble of phoning your mother and asking her to think of possible addresses; you rushed round to the most likely one in your dinner-hour, and then, when you found that there was a woman visitor staying there, you simply dropped the whole thing?" he asked.

" Yes," said Larry defiantly. But he was beginning to look worried.

" Mrs. Anslow was not expecting you to give up," Burbage pointed out. " She told Mrs. Pole that you would be coming back."

" She was mistaken; I didn't," said Larry.

" Why not?"

" The whole thing began to seem silly," said Larry. " I only have an hour for lunch. Two days running I'd had a job to get back to work in time. I was going to be in trouble for getting in late. It didn't seem worth it."

" So, after straining heaven and earth to find Mrs. Anslow, at the moment when you found her, you decided to give up for ever?" repeated Burbage.

" That's right," said Larry.

Even to Celia, who longed to believe him, it sounded so lame as to be insulting.

" Then, if someone said that you were there at the same

time next day, you would deny it?" said Burbage.

" Of course," said Larry.

He answered confidently, but he could not resist adding, in a dismayed voice,

" Who says I was there?"

" I was simply asking you to clarify your part in what happened," said Burbage.

It had been a try-on; no one had actually seen Larry return, Celia deduced. Burbage had hoped to make him betray himself. But she could find no fault with Burbage's behaviour after that. He said that he was grateful to Larry for his help; he hoped that if Larry or Celia remembered anything else that might be useful they would let him know. If either of them came across Mrs. Anslow again they should inform her that the police also wished her to get in touch with them. They had to get to the bottom of this assault business. He himself would not be idle. Then he got up to go.

When Larry came back from seeing Burbage out there was silence for a long moment. Celia was hesitating. She was an ardent reader of magazine stories, and she had always marvelled at the heroine who would not ask her fiancé why he was kissing the elegant blonde, but instead rushed off to be a governess somewhere, putting him to untold effort to discover her again, and explain that the blonde was his long-lost sister. Why, why, would heroines not ask? Celia used to demand.

Now she knew. The heroine did not ask, because just so long as she had not asked, and her true love had not answered, she could go on believing that he would not lie to her. Celia had given way to panic, before, over the blue rabbit. Once again she was tempted, sorely tempted, to pretend that there was nothing troubling her at all. But this time commonsense prevailed. She asked: and listened to Larry's answer.

NINETEEN

LARRY SAID that he had not waited for Mrs. Pole to answer the door because he knew that if he stayed to talk for even three minutes he would be late back to work. He said that when he arrived at the office, out of breath, and ravenously hungry, not having had time to eat a bite of his sandwiches, or snatch a cup of tea at the canteen, the futility of the whole thing suddenly struck him. If he went back again that would make three days when he had had no proper lunch break; it wasn't worth it.

Celia weighed the answer, and, hard though she tried, she found it wanting. She couldn't forget Larry's obsessive interest, his unnatural persistence, his unnatural silence. She could not believe that he would give up so near the goal. But if he had gone back to Eastfold Street, what had he done there, that he could not admit to it? Her mind shied away from the answer.

"Why didn't you tell me that you'd been to Mrs. Pole's house?" she asked.

"I thought it would worry you," Larry replied virtuously.

Once again Celia found it hard to believe him.

" Why should it worry me?" she asked.

" I could tell that you didn't like me to keep on at Iris. You thought it was her I was interested in, I know," Larry answered.

It was true enough, but Celia was put out that Larry should have known it. She had imagined she was being so sympathetic, so loving and tactful. Her hurt prompted her next words.

" You ought to have told me that you had brought her back to sleep here, that first night," she said.

" I was afraid that would worry you, too," Larry said. " But she suddenly told me at the bus-stop that she was afraid to go back into town, because of the shock she'd had earlier. She was trembling all over; she didn't seem in a condition even to get on the bus. But after I'd brought her back I worried all night. Fortunately I knew it was all right, the next morning. I gave her some breakfast with mine, and I could tell that she was perfectly normal again."

" How?" said Celia starkly.

" Oh, I don't know. The way she behaved. She told me off for not warming the teapot when I was making your tea."

Larry grinned.

It was a fair enough test of normality, Celia agreed. Yet she herself had seemed to see two people in Iris, one who made perfect toast, and was in full control of her actions, inviting no interference; and one who seemed haunted.

Celia was in the dilemma now of those who have asked and got an answer. She wanted to believe Larry, but she was not sure that she could.

Nothing more was said about Iris Anslow that evening, nor for the next few days. Tacitly they decided to let the subject rest. The visit of Burbage had one unforeseen result, however. Celia's neighbours, who were never there when they might have been of use, nor ever saw anything that they were wanted to see, seemed somehow to have noticed Burbage's call, and to have sensed that he was an enquiry agent. They eyed Celia and Larry askance, and were even more aloof than usual.

In the village, little was changed. The stares continued. But Flora Anslow now waved from behind her curtain. She had probably decided that she would have to be friendly, because she and the Riddells were in the same boat, Celia decided. Burbage and the police must be interested in both of them.

Bill Anslow, that ardent gardener, was invisible, however. Though the weather was not cold, he was not doing his digging.

This state of things went on until the next Saturday afternoon. And then, just as Celia was washing up after lunch, there was a commotion at the kitchen door, and Flora Anslow came rushing through.

Her face was absolutely colourless, her eyes starting out of her head. She moved as if someone unseen was jerking strings. She looked at Celia, saw Larry behind her, and gave a sigh of relief.

" Mr. Riddell! Come quickly! " she said. " Someone has been digging in our garden. Bill won't have it, but I think they've done for Iris, and buried her."

Celia was looking at Larry. She saw him grow old before her eyes. She herself aged immeasurably as she envisaged all the possibilities.

Larry seemed rooted to the spot. Flora Anslow, however, was charged with feverish energy.

" Come on! Come quickly," she urged.

Larry moved, very slowly.

" Better go and look, I suppose," he said to Celia, avoiding her eyes.

She went to him, and took his hand and squeezed it, trying to convey all her love and loyalty. But he seemed not to understand.

" We shall have to go," he said.

He led the way out of the kitchen. To Celia's horror, he did not ask where to go, but made for the path behind the pigsties. Would Flora remember later that Larry had not asked where the grave was, that he seemed already to know?

" Where is it?" Celia asked loudly.

Flora answered impatiently.

" In our garden. By our back hedge. Oh hurry, please hurry."

If Iris Anslow was dead and buried, a few minutes' delay would presumably not worry her. Larry was running, however, so Celia urged her heavy legs along, too. They skirted the pigsties, squeezed through the gap between the oak tree and the hazel bush, and stumbled along the cart-track in the field. When they reached the corner cottage garden they had only to step over a low fence.

The place was shielded from the field and the cottage by privet hedges. It was next to Bill Anslow's compost heap. Bill Anslow was standing looking down.

There was a shallow depression in the moss-covered earth. Even Celia could tell that the small oblong of fresh earth was in ground that had not been turned over for at least a year. She looked at it in horror and fascination. She had no doubt that Iris Anslow was down there. For some reason she thought of her not as a putrefying mass, but as a neat heap of white bones, grinning just below the surface of the soil.

Larry broke the silence.

"Have you told the police?" he asked anxiously.

Bill shook his head.

"Why should they bury her in our garden?" Flora burst out. "If someone has done Iris in, why should they bring her to us?"

"Anyone could get in from the field," said Larry.

"But why try to put the blame on us? Bill had nothing to do with it. He's been kept in the house with bronchitis. The doctor told him it was more than his life was worth to put his nose into the garden," said Flora. "He hasn't had a spade in his hand for weeks; I can prove it."

"No one is going to blame you," said Larry soothingly.

"Oh, yes, they will, if they can. It will all have to come out now, you'll see," said Flora tearfully.

Celia also was mourning, but she was too tense for tears. Larry seemed the calmest of them all.

"You haven't disturbed the ground at any time yourself?" he asked Bill.

How could Larry sound so business-like? But Bill seemed grateful.

"Not for years," he replied. "Nothing grows near this damned privet. But I leave it in to keep us a bit private from people going up and down the field."

"Do you know when this was done?" Larry asked.

"No. It wasn't here a few weeks ago, that's all I know. As Flora told you, I've been shut up in the house."

" Anyone could step in from the field without disturbing you, and make a hole unseen, if they knew where to dig. And anyone who went up and down the field would know that," said Larry.

They all stood looking down for an infinity more. Then Larry exclaimed suddenly.

" It's a very small grave! " Strangely, the idea seemed to terrify him.

Flora gave a wail.

" Iris wasn't a big woman," she said.

" But she was surely five feet? " Larry said.

" Perhaps," suggested Flora, shuddering all over, " they have chopped her up? "

The two men gazed at each other. They did not contradict the suggestion.

" We might as well look and see? " said Larry.

" The police? " suggested Bill Anslow.

" I can't wait for them, can you? " said Larry.

" The clues? " said Bill faintly.

" The hell with the clues," said Larry violently. " I'm going to have a look."

TWENTY

IF LARRY thought that there was something to be gained by destroying clues, Celia was not going to stop him. The other two did not protest, either. They looked scared, horror-struck, but excited. Larry knelt down, and with his fingers began gently to scoop off the soil.

He worked without apparent effect for a few moments, then drew his head back with a horrified exclamation.

" There is something here! " he said. " I touched something then. Something that gave . . . something soft, and, well, fleshy . . ."

" Leave it alone," Celia begged.

" I can't do that now," Larry replied.

Although he had gone pale he continued to push away the soil with his fingers, as gingerly as if he were an archaeologist excavating. But he had an easier task. After only a second something emerged to sight. To Celia's horror it was recognisably human, a pale pinkish-grey obscenely naked throat.

Flora gave a long moan, and clutched Celia's arm. Bill stood looking aghast. Larry had straightened his back, still on his knees, staring down.

" Who could have killed poor Iris?" Flora moaned.

" That's not a person! " Larry exclaimed.

Celia saw at once what he meant. Human flesh, buried for weeks, would not be that revolting naked pink. She shuddered to think what it really would look like, but the relief flooding over her was too great to linger on the idea.

" Is it a statue, then?" she asked wonderingly.

" No, not a statue," Larry answered. " It's soft." He shuddered in his turn. " It feels horrible," he complained, flexing his fingers, but then he went back to work vigorously. In a minute more he was able to grip and heave. The thing came flying out at their feet.

" It's a dressmaker's dummy! " Celia exclaimed.

" Somebody's idea of a joke," said Larry, his face disgusted.

But Bill and Flora remained tense.

" Don't you recognise it?" Flora asked Bill in a low voice. " It's Maudie, our Maudie."

" It must be very old," said Celia, marvelling. " They don't make them to look like real people nowadays."

" It is old," said Flora. " It was my grandmother's. We called it Maudie just because it looked human. My mother never liked us to leave Maudie about where people could see her. We had to keep a cover on her, too, a jacket-lining that had never been finished."

" Why is she here, then?" asked Larry.

" She was up in the roof, I know," Flora said. " We didn't use her much, and when Bill and I were clearing out, after Dad died, we put Maudie up in the loft with the other things we didn't want, and didn't quite like to throw away. In case Maud, my sister-in-law, Iris's mother, came back, you know. Mother had given Maudie to her."

" Then what fool buried her here?" asked Larry.

" It could have been Iris herself," said Celia, trying to make amends for what she had imagined, by a rush of harmless explanations. " She went up into the roof. And then I heard her go to the toolhouse. I remember now. She could have been getting a spade. She could have brought the dummy here and buried it. She had the time."

" But what did she do it for?" asked Larry. " Is it her idea of a joke?"

" Iris wouldn't play jokes like that," said Flora definitely.

" Then she must have gone dotty," stated Larry.

" Iris isn't dotty; she's got a very good head," said Flora, unaccountably offended.

Bill nodded gloomily.

" Then what did she do it for? To scare us?" demanded Larry.

There was a baffled silence.

" They don't make them like that any more," repeated Celia.

" It's covered with kid, pink kid," complained Larry.

" Where's her jacket?" asked Flora. " Mother wouldn't let us carry Maudie about without her jacket."

Larry bent to the hole again and retrieved a folded dirty rag. It must have slid off as he pulled the dummy out. He shook the rag out now, and it fell into a recognisable shape. It was a waisted jacket, made of a stiff material which had been silvery grey.

" It's a lining. We used to make our own suits and coats. People don't any more," Flora said. " The material is very old. They don't make material to last like that any more, either."

" I shouldn't regret it," muttered Larry. " These seams are as hard as iron. It would have taken your skin off."

" It's a jacket lining," said Flora, affronted. " You didn't wear them on your bare skin."

" What's this bit?" asked Larry, touching a piece of dirty canvas.

" Stiffening for the lapels."

" And this?" He was holding a tiny bag of material.

" That's a weight, to hold the hem down. There should be two, one for each side of the front."

" My mother used to stitch a threepenny bit into her dress hems, to keep them down," volunteered Celia.

" This isn't a threepenny bit, worse luck," said Larry.

" Oh, no, the weights were just lumps of lead. You bought

them specially," explained Flora. " They didn't have a hole in, so they had to be covered, and stitched in place."

" This isn't a lump of lead, either," remarked Larry.

He worked at the bag with his fingers. Damp had affected the material; it had begun to rot. He forced out the weight quite easily, and even before he rubbed it on his sleeve it shone dully with reddish gold.

" I do believe it's a gold sovereign! " Larry exclaimed.

They crowded round, leaving Maudie forgotten by the compost heap.

" That's what it is! " Bill agreed.

" Let me see," begged Celia.

She looked with pleasure at the design of St. George and the dragon, which she had never seen before.

" One? There should be a hundred," said Flora sharply.

Bill bent and began to sift the earth from the hole. But he soon gave up. It was plain that there had been nothing else buried there in Maudie's grave.

" The other weight, then? Is that a sovereign too?" asked Flora.

Larry had difficulty in finding another weight. The reason became clear when he produced the second little bag. It had been slit open. Whatever it had contained was gone.

" No luck, I'm afraid," he said to Flora.

She was deep in thought.

" This is Iris's doing," she announced at last. " She put Maudie here, and the sovereign. It's here because it's mine. Iris wasn't going to keep it, or let anyone else take it, but she wasn't going to give it to me, either."

" No, she isn't mad," Flora went on, crossly, looking up, and meeting Celia's expressive eyes. " Iris is honest, that's all. We said she must have taken the sovereigns, and she

was offended. She didn't say she hadn't, because she thought
we ought to have known better. But she must have found
these two. She took her mother's share, and put mine where
it belonged, in our garden. She wasn't going to give it to
me, after what I'd said, but if we found it, we found it, and
if we didn't, it was meant. This is Iris's doing, all right.
She wouldn't care what trouble she went to, so long as she
didn't have to give me the sovereign herself."

Celia's eyes found Larry's, and expressed her unchanged
opinion of Iris's mentality.

"What about the other ninety-eight?" he asked.

"Dad will have sold them," stated Flora. "It was never
legal to keep them, you know, but his own father had always
had a gold sovereign in his pocket. Old people didn't like
them being done away with. But Dad must have had to part
with them when money was getting tight. He must have kept
one each back for Maud and me, as souvenirs. That was like
him. He wasn't always kind to us, but he was fair. There
was no sense in putting two sovereigns back in the hiding-
place under the floor. He needed to be able to get at them.
Mom probably sewed them up in Maudie's jacket straightaway. Then, when she had to go into hospital, she forgot
all about them. They're just a nuisance now, after all, not
like ready money . . . Yes, that's what happened. But Iris
wouldn't say. She's stubborn. I had no business thinking
she'd taken them; Iris wouldn't do a thing like that."

"No," said Bill. "Iris wouldn't."

"You didn't say that at the time," said Flora sharply.

"No," said Bill regretfully. "Somehow, when it comes
to money . . . you can't feel sure . . . It seems as if anyone
might do anything. But you're right. Iris wouldn't make off
with money that belonged to you and her mother, even if

it was a secret, and there was no one left to tax her with it. Iris wouldn't do a thing like that."

" She may not be a thief, but she's given me a horrible shock," complained Larry. " It's a good thing the neighbours didn't hear your wife saying what we were expecting to find. They would never have believed that there wasn't something in it."

" A good thing you wouldn't wait for the police, too! " exclaimed Bill. " We should have looked a couple of fools! "

" What we all want is a nice cup of tea," said Flora briskly. " If you'll come inside, I'll get us one. The kettle's on the boil."

TWENTY-ONE

CELIA WOULD have preferred to be alone with Larry, so that she could begin making amends to him at once for having thought that if Iris Anslow had been murdered he might have had a hand in it. But Larry, she could see, was eager to accept Flora's offer. It would have been an anticlimax, she had to admit, to part without another word, so they all trooped into the cottage.

This time Larry and Celia were given the freedom of the kitchen. It was as cosy as the front room, but darker. The kettle was singing on a trivet by the side of the coal fire. The cat was snoring on the rug. Larry and Celia sank into the two comfortable armchairs, and felt remarkably at home.

Over tea they talked, pairing off, so that Bill and Larry were discussing football and the garden, and Flora and Celia shops and house-cleaning. And Iris. Flora admitted, in a low voice, trying to keep the men from hearing her, that she was worried about Iris. Not because she still thought anything dreadful had happened, but because Iris had been in an unfriendly mood, and Flora was always uneasy when she felt that Iris was hating her.

" Iris was always so energetic," she explained. " She gave her whole mind to anything she was doing, or thinking. And so obstinate! You could never get an idea out of her head once she had got it in."

" Do you suppose she got in a temper with Mrs. Pole, then, and walked out?" said Celia. " And was too proud to go back for her things?"

" I don't know what to think," said Flora. " I shouldn't have thought anything at all if that man hadn't come round asking questions, on behalf of a well-wisher, he said. They make the things people do sound too ' meant,' don't they? Everybody has their own little ways, after all—I mean, like me always watching the people get off the bus, and happening to notice Iris, and sending Bill after her to see why she hadn't come back. Of course I knew where she must have gone! Where else would she be going? And of course I hadn't known she was coming. I can look out of my window without having to be on the watch for my niece, that I haven't seen for years, surely?"

" Of course," said Celia soothingly, for Flora was getting so agitated that she was dribbling her tea.

" That man who came round was no good at all," Flora

announced. "He should be looking for the criminal, not visiting Iris's relations, and trying to make them say that she wasn't right in the head. He'll never find out anything, you'll see."

Brave words, but Flora had to eat them almost immediately, for as they were finishing their second cup of tea, Burbage rang the front door bell.

He still looked worn out, but his eyes were jubilant.

"What a piece of luck to find you all together!" he exclaimed, though with a hint in his voice that it was really rather odd, and probably meant that they were up to something. "It saves me a journey," he went on, nodding across to Larry. "I thought you'd all like to know that Mrs. Anslow, wherever she may be, is in the clear. The police got to the bottom of the attack on Mrs. Pole. Got a confession."

"Who was it?" asked Larry.

"The Jamaican who lived in the house across the street."

"A Jamaican!" Larry gave a whistle. "That won't do the colour problem any good," he said.

"No. Though I must say Mrs. Pole is being surprisingly broadminded," Burbage said. "She doesn't seem to bear him a grudge about the actual attempt to throttle her. Seems to take the line that doing a little thing like that might happen to anybody. No, what she takes exception to is the way he called on her when he repented and told her, 'I sorry.' 'Why can't they speak proper English?' she keeps saying."

"Who was he? What on earth did he do it for?" asked Larry.

"He lodges in the front room across the way, with a woman friend. It appears he had a grudge against Mrs. Pole because she wouldn't take him and his woman in. He didn't mind too much, until he found out that she was putting up Mrs. Anslow. That did annoy him. And it seems that on the day in question he got up to his lunch—he works nights—and he hadn't had any sleep because of the kids in the house screaming, and his woman was yelling at him that it was his own fault for not finding anywhere better to live, and it all got too much for him, and he rushed across to have a row with Mrs. Pole. He found the front door open and darted in, and did his best to throttle her. Fortunately, he came to himself in time, and fled the same way he had come. But one of his pals saw him, and gossip began to get around, and he thought it might look better if he owned up and said he was sorry, before the police found out. Pass it off as just a slip, so to speak."

"He's no right to go round doing things like that," said Flora, with a disapproving frown.

"Not gentlemanly," nodded Burbage.

"You may laugh," Flora said, flushing. "But it isn't right."

"I wasn't laughing," said Burbage hastily. "It most certainly is not the right way to behave, and he's very lucky that it didn't turn out to be serious. Mrs. Pole is not a young woman, and her heart might not have stood up to the shock. No, I'm not trying to minimise what he did. But at least we know the truth. Any news of Mrs. Anslow?"

"No," they all said.

"Well, the police won't be concerning themselves any more. I'm on my own," said Burbage.

He took himself off.

When he had gone, Larry and Celia got up to go. But they did not leave at once.

" It's all very well," said Flora in a dissatisfied voice. " You see, the police don't care anything now about poor Iris. If they can't accuse her of trying to strangle somebody, they won't even look for her."

" She is quite safe somewhere," said Bill consolingly.

" I'm not sure she is," said Flora.

" I don't think she is, either," said Larry unexpectedly. " I think she ought to be found."

Celia was still so dazed with relief that she would have agreed with anything Larry said, but at this she could not help an impatient sigh.

" If she doesn't want to be found . . ." she murmured.

" We don't know that she doesn't," said Larry obstinately. " All we know is that she went off. Perhaps she was the one who couldn't stand the shock? Perhaps this man also attacked her, but nobody knows, so he isn't saying anything?"

" I shouldn't think that's very likely," said Bill.

" I don't, myself," admitted Larry. " But we don't know, do we? And nobody seems to care, unless Mrs. Pole still does. I think Iris ought to be found."

" Us put a detective on her, you mean?" asked Bill, frowning slightly. " Pay that Burbage?"

" How could we afford a detective?" asked Larry impatiently. " No, I'll be my own detective. I'll find her myself, if you'll give me some help."

" What do you want us to do?" asked Bill.

" Well, in the first place," said Larry. " What is it that makes her do a bolt? Why did she leave the first time, when she ran away from The Red House?"

" That hasn't got anything to do with anything," said Flora in a suddenly hostile voice.

Larry was not offended by her tone. To Celia he seemed rather to be pleased.

" I think it has," he replied. " I think that what happened then has a great deal to do with what has happened now."

" It was years ago! " said Bill mildly.

" I still think that there is a connection," said Larry obstinately.

Bill and Flora exchanged uneasy glances. Celia could have told them that they would make no headway against Larry when he had a conviction. They were middle-aged and tired, and his eager thrusting youth fatigued them even more. They gave way, a little, not knowing that it was fatal, that they would find themselves giving way again and again .

" She wasn't well, then," Flora said. " She was in such a queer state of mind that Bill was worried about her."

TWENTY-TWO

FLORA LOOKED at Bill. He made a defeated gesture, and turned away from all of them.

" If Iris didn't mind talking about it, why should you?" he said, staring into the fire. " It's a long time ago, after all. What does it matter, any more?"

" I don't see what good it's going to do," said Flora,

but she took Bill's speech as permission to talk. And once she began she was glad to let it all loose; the words came tumbling out.

" It was Keith," she declared. " He upset all the girls. And he made a dead set at Iris, because he knew my Dad wouldn't like it. Wouldn't like it! He would have burst with rage, if he'd had the slightest suspicion! Iris was with Keith when she was supposed to be at the Technical College in the evenings, and sometimes they'd come back to The Red House by the fields without letting on. Iris made them a place in the loft above the sties. Dad could still walk in those days, but he couldn't get up the ladder, so they were quite safe, and quite comfortable. Not that there was anything really wrong, of course. Maud wouldn't have let Iris go wrong.

" I don't know how it would all have turned out if Keith hadn't gone to sea. Keith went off to his ship, and he didn't come home on leave. We hardly knew where he was any more. Until the news came that he was lost in the China seas. And then Iris married Bill."

Celia fought to control her expression at this point. She felt all the embarrassment that Flora and Bill ought to have been feeling. Flora seemed to understand, for she explained quickly, " It was Maud's doing. She said it was for Mother's sake, and Dad's. Maud was in a sanatorium, then; she's still there. Dad was only able to move from his chair to his bed and back again, by then, but Mother was still active. Only, she'd gone a bit childish and forgetful; you couldn't trust her to look after herself, let alone Dad. They'd have starved or burnt to death, left to themselves, yet they were terrified at the idea of being sent away somewhere. But Maud didn't want me to get married, when she hadn't a husband herself any more. So she married Iris to Bill.

"Dad had all his faculties still, and he wouldn't have allowed it, if he had known. He would have died sooner. So they kept it dark. Mother knew, though. She was pleased, and it was the sort of secret that she could still keep. Bill was working on the land, because of his weak chest, and he was gone from first light to dark. He came and went by the field, and if there was anyone visiting the house he often stayed out in the loft. If Dad heard his voice, Mother used to pretend that he was the man calling for the newspaper money. The neighbours had their own troubles to think about; and if they suspected anything, they wouldn't have dared tell Dad."

"Then what made her run off?" asked Larry.

"Keith came home. We never knew what they said to each other; Bill was away at work. When he got back in the evening Iris had gone, and the whole house was wide open. Dad had a stroke that night, so he never missed Iris at all, and Mother was so ill, because of Dad, that she had to go into hospital, too. They had to let me come home. Iris never wrote. She didn't come back for the funerals. We never saw her again, until she got off the bus a few weeks ago."

"Keith didn't go after her?" asked Larry.

"Oh, no. Keith never needed to go after any girl. They all came to him," said Flora. "He went to London for the rest of his leave, but of course, he had to go back to sea again afterwards. He was never ship-wrecked again, though. He settled in Australia. We never heard where Iris went."

"She went to my mother," said Larry.

"Zelda!" exclaimed Flora. "All that misery and worry, and poor Bill worrying and wondering, and Zelda Wright had Iris with her all the time! And never let us know! She had no business to do such a thing! She ought to be put in gaol! "

" She did it for the best," said Larry.

" It wasn't for the best at all. But it was exactly like her. Exactly! Pushing, bossy, knowing what everybody ought to do better than they did themselves. And making a mess of their lives for them," said Flora.

Larry let her run herself down.

Then he said, " Iris had no reason to complain. If she had to run away, she couldn't have gone to a better place."

" It was so . . . so officious of Zelda! " complained Flora, absurdly.

" Let it rest," commanded Bill unexpectedly. " Zelda must have thought she was acting for the best, as the boy says."

Flora subsided.

Larry looked across at Bill Anslow.

" I shall find Iris again," he said.

" If you say so," said Bill. His voice held no pleasure, and he went back to staring into the fire.

" How you can be so calm! " said Flora to him piteously. " I feel ill! It's been like a nightmare, but now that it's over, I feel worse than ever."

" You'll be better after a good night's sleep," said Larry consolingly. " Which reminds me, we ought to be getting home. The fire will be out."

" You want to be careful, in that great cold house," said Flora.

" We'll be careful," said Larry. " Come on, Celia."

They went to the door, making for the back door, like intimates of the house.

"See you again soon," Larry said, in the most natural way. He took Celia's hand, and they hurried across the garden, past Maudie lying forsaken on the compost heap, and over the fence into the field. They had to slow down on the cart-track, which was too rough for running, but they hurried through their own hedge. Celia was weak with gratitude to the fates which had prevented her from giving away to Larry her ugly fears about him. So she refrained from saying that she thought Bill Anslow had behaved like the village half-wit. What if Iris was a hysterical personality, who gave him hell? He should have alerted the police, and Zelda would have been forced to come forward. But Larry's thoughts were still on Iris.

"We'll have to find out how solicitors trace missing persons," he remarked. "There must be a routine way of going about it."

"Oh, Larry, must we?" asked Celia. "Now we know all this, why don't we let her alone? She probably wants just that. Wouldn't it be better to leave things as they are?"

"No," replied Larry.

But he said it, Celia was glad to observe, without the slightest hint of strain. He was himself again. Finding Iris was a job he had set himself, from which nothing Celia could say would deflect him. But he meant her to share in his efforts, this time. She had to be thankful for that.

All evening Larry broke into whatever they were doing or saying with some idea which had just occurred to him. But next morning, when he woke up, it seemed that he had come to the conclusion in sleeping that the first thing to do was to interview Mrs. Pole.

"She must have some idea why a woman who was lodging

with her should suddenly up and go," Larry said. " I don't care what she told the police, she must have some idea. It isn't as if Iris was a stranger. She had stayed with Mrs. Pole before. Mrs. Pole was a sort of unofficial aunt to the Belmonts, my mother said. You can't tell me that an un-official aunt hasn't some theory about where Iris has gone."

Nothing would content Larry but that they should call on Mrs. Pole that very day. But he agreed that it would be politic to wait till late afternoon, when she would pre-sumably have risen refreshed from her afternoon nap.

Larry and Celia went by bus into town. As they waited at the bus stop, they waved to Flora. Bill got up from some-where at the back of the room, and stood and signalled to them, too. Then the bus came, and they were wafted apart. In town, Larry and Celia went on foot to Eastfold Street.

It was quite a broad pleasant street. The houses were about eighty years old, and wearing well but, the soot of years seemed to have collected in the black tunnels of the entries.

" Shall we knock at the front door, or go round to the back?" asked Larry.

They came to the conclusion, quite rightly, as it turned out, that Mrs. Pole would prefer them to go round the back, where she could inspect them at leisure before she let them in, without the whole street looking on.

There was no difficulty, actually, in getting admitted. Though Mrs. Pole was an independent old lady she was also a very lonely one. Visitors of any sort were a delight to her. It was easier, after Larry and Celia had met her, and sensed what her life must be, to understand why the Jamaican's attack had not turned her into a nervous wreck. It would have been an exaggeration, of course, to say that she welcomed even people who rushed in and tried to throttle her, but it made a change.

Larry and Celia began by explaining who they were. It was sufficient to say that Larry was Zelda Riddell's son. Mrs. Pole threw the door open to them, and announced that the kettle was on.

They filed in, through the scullery, into the warm kitchen. Mrs. Pole sat them down round the fire, where she could see their faces, and busied herself with setting out cups. She moved with difficulty because of rheumatism, and her head trembled occasionally, but her large pale face was calm, and her hoarse voice assured.

"I knew your mother well when she was Zelda Wright," she said to Larry.

"Bossy, interfering, knowing everybody's business better than they did themselves," recited Larry resignedly.

Mrs. Pole gave an appreciative chuckle. "That was Zelda to the life," she said. "But I'm surprised you shouldn't mind saying so."

"Oh, I don't think it's offensive. I'm bossy, too," said Larry. He grinned at Celia. "Mother can't intimidate me," he said. "We're two of a kind. She was dead against our buying The Red House. Prophesied all sorts of woe. But we did it, and we're very satisfied. Aren't we, Celia?"

"I liked old-fashioned houses," Celia said.

"What was the matter? Did Zelda think it would be damp?" Mrs. Pole asked, as she poured boiling water into the teapot.

"I think she had some idea that it was not a happy house," said Larry.

It was a cue, but Mrs. Pole did not take it. She put down

the kettle, and fitted the teapot lid on the pot with care and concentration. Larry looked at Celia, and changed the subject.

"We were very sorry to hear about the man who came in and attacked you," he said. "It must have given you a dreadful shock."

"Oh, him," said Mrs. Pole contemptuously.

"I hope there's been no more trouble?" said Larry.

"I look through him when I see him in the street," Mrs. Pole said. "I don't say anything, but he knows what I mean by it, all right. I shan't have any bother from him again."

"I'm very glad to hear it," murmured Larry, while Celia was struggling not to laugh.

"He isn't married to that woman, you know," went on Mrs. Pole. "He calls her his wife, but she isn't. And he had the nerve to expect me to take them in!"

TWENTY-THREE

CELIA WONDERED whether Mrs. Pole knew about Bill and Flora Anslow, and whether she felt the same indignation. Very probably, she thought, but it was impossible to ask. It could have been by telepathy that Mrs. Pole was moved to say next,

" We were half expecting you to call when Iris Anslow was here."

" We would have done, if she had given us the address," said Larry.

" She never got round to it," said Mrs. Pole.

" She was intending to let us know she was here, then?" asked Larry.

" Oh, yes, I think so. She said you were the worrying sort. She said you would never leave people to themselves. Like Zelda."

" I hope she meant that kindly," said Larry.

" Oh, I'm sure of it," said Mrs. Pole apologetically. " Yes, of course she meant it kindly."

" And did she need help?" asked Larry bluntly.

Mrs. Pole laid her cup down.

" I was worried about her," she admitted. " I am still."

" What makes you worry?"

" She wasn't herself, at all."

" She seemed to be feeling better when she left us," said Larry, looking to Celia for confirmation.

" I thought she was quite calm and settled in her mind," said Celia.

" She wasn't herself," said Mrs. Pole. The sudden trembling of her head emphasised her anxiety.

" Did she go to a doctor?" asked Larry.

" She wasn't ill! "

" Are you sure?" Larry asked. " She had had an accident in town, hadn't she, the day she came to The Red House. Couldn't it be that she had mild concussion from it, and didn't realise it?"

" I suppose it could," said Mrs. Pole doubtfully. " But it wasn't that sort of accident, was it?"

" What sort of accident was it, then?" asked Larry.

" She'd met someone unexpectedly; it was suddenly seeing him that did for her," said Mrs. Pole. " Made her walk into a parked car."

" Keith Anslow, was that?" asked Larry keenly.

" Did she tell you, then?"

" No. I've just guessed."

" Bill and Flora never hear from him at all," Mrs. Pole said. " I'm sure they've got no idea where he is, or that he's come back home. And Iris never thought to meet him again. She liked to pretend he was dead. It was like seeing a ghost, she said. She wasn't sure whether he'd seen her, but it was walking away from him, not looking where she was going, that caused the accident. He'd moved on by then. Trust him not to be about when he could have given a hand, though he's always there to stir up trouble."

" You don't like him, then?" asked Larry.

" I don't know him, not to say know. But what I've heard about him is enough. Mind you, the only time I saw him, I could understand how he got the way he is. He was handsome all right. And he had a way with him. For two pins he would have made love to me, old as I was, and for two pins I would have let him. Of course, he had charm. Always cheerful. But a great big smile was all he ever gave anyone. No thought for anything but Keith Anslow, no human kindness, no morals. Take Bill, and think of the exact opposite, and you've got Keith."

" That's very interesting," said Larry.

" More sinned against than sinning, I always say about poor Bill Anslow," said Mrs. Pole defiantly, making it plain at last that Bill's and Flora's situation was perfectly well known to her.

" I'm sure you're right," answered Larry politely. He put down his empty cup, ready for business.

" Do you know where Iris Anslow is?" he asked.

" No. I told the police."

" But was that the truth?"

" It was," said Mrs. Pole, unoffended.

" Haven't you any idea where she went?"

" I haven't the least idea why she went! " exclaimed Mrs. Pole. " I'm worried sick about it. Iris would never go off like that of her own free will. Never."

" But she had done it before," Larry pointed out.

" No, she never had."

" She went away from The Red House just as suddenly, before her parents died."

" That was different," declared Mrs. Pole.

" I suppose we shall never know why she went that time, either," said Larry in a resigned voice. " No one has any idea."

His assertion acted on Mrs. Pole like a challenge.

" It depends what you mean by ' no one '. I know very well why she went," she said.

" Really?" Larry's whole figure tautened with expectation, but he put polite doubt into his voice.

" That was her precious brother-in-law's doing, too," Mrs. Pole said.

" Really?" Larry murmured again. His voice, like a cooing dove's, was designed not to jar on Mrs. Pole, nor interrupt her train of thought.

" He called on Iris when he found she was married to Bill, and gave her his plans for his leave," Mrs. Pole said, indignant colour blotching her wrinkled face. " His idea was that he should slip in and spend the afternoons with her, and then, when Bill came home in the evening, they would all three go off to the pubs together as if nothing had happened. I know, because Iris told me. And I know she was horrified, because she told me so. She wasn't like the rest of you young people nowadays. The idea of carrying on with her husband's brother while her husband was out at work, and then behaving when he came back as if it meant nothing at all, was disgusting to her. So, do you know what he said, to persuade her? 'Don't worry about Bill,' he said 'I've thrown him in the cut.' And he described it so well, how Bill struggled, and drowned, and just a few bubbles came up, that Iris ran off, without stopping to do more than pick up her handbag and suchlike, and never dared to write home, or look in a paper for months. She knew Keith, none better, and she knew that somehow or other he usually managed to get his way."

"So that was how it was," said Larry.

"It means nothing to you," asserted Mrs. Pole. "But Maud and Flora had been properly taught, and they brought Iris up right. She wasn't brought up to all the chopping and changing, with no one thinking anything of it, that goes on nowadays. Iris told me that it came to her that day that Keith was a devil, and she meant every word of it. You can laugh as much as you like; that's how she felt, and how any decent girl would have felt, in my day."

"We are not laughing," said Larry.

Mrs. Pole grew calmer. "No, no, of course, you wouldn't," she apologised. "I shouldn't have said that. I'm sure any boy of Zelda's would be a decent lad, and I'm sure you married a decent girl, too. I'm worried about Iris, that's the trouble. I thought that keeping house for a clergyman, the way she did, she would have been settled in life, grown out of her troubles, by now. But I got the feeling that it was all beginning all over again, and I didn't like it."

" Do you think that Keith Anslow knew that she was with you?" asked Larry.

" I don't know. But if he had found out somehow, he knew I wouldn't have let him into the house," said Mrs. Pole. " Besides, if he did see her that day, he surely thinks of it as all over long ago. He'll have had half a dozen other girls since those days. No, it's what Iris is doing that worries me. I've thought and thought, but I can't see any reason for her to go off like that."

Mrs. Pole had worked herself up into a state of distress. She looked every hour of her age. Celia and Larry had to set about soothing her, with assurances that everything would be all right, that it would all turn out to have been worry about nothing, she would see.

The assurances had no foundation, and Mrs. Pole knew it, but the mere automatic murmuring of them helped her. Larry and Celia dosed her with sympathy every few seconds as if it were brandy and sugar in spoonfuls, and it gave her back the strength to calm herself deliberately. She told them that she knew that she must not upset herself, for she was too old to stand it. So one moment she was still keening for Iris, with a voice that shook, and eyes that streamed; the next, she was warming the tea-pot again, with not a thought in the world but her own survival.

TWENTY-FOUR

LARRY AND Celia refused more tea, but lingered while Mrs. Pole sipped hers. They were appalled by what they had done to her. It was not till she gave a sharp exclamation, and sprang to her feet, hobbling across the room and throwing up the window to shout at the neighbour's cat, who was nonchalantly scraping up earth among her primulas, that they felt reassured enough to leave. Mrs. Pole thanked them for their visit, and urged them to come again, and they thanked her, and promised that they would. Then they escaped, with a profound sense of release, into the smoky grey late afternoon.

They took hands as they walked up the little street, where most of the other strollers were black.

" I'm afraid it was a waste of time, after all. You won't have got any ideas from that. Poor old thing! " said Celia.

" I've got the only idea I need," said Larry.

" What's that?"

" To find Keith Anslow."

" But he can't have anything to do with it, now! "

" Every time she has run away, she has been running from him," said Larry. " She couldn't bring herself to go

E

to Mrs. Pole's that first night, in case he had come to look for her there."

"But he hasn't been to Mrs. Pole's!"

"If he has been there, Mrs. Pole doesn't know," corrected Larry. "But she can't even say exactly when Iris went. Suppose Keith Anslow knew of several places where Iris might be staying, and took a stroll one day down East-fold Street. He could have enquired, and been told by some ignorant or malicious person that there was no one staying with Mrs. Pole. Or he could have made sure Iris was there, gone away again, intending to come back. But Iris could have seen him, or heard about him, and could have decided that she must get away at once. And then he asked Burbage to find her. Mrs. Pole didn't do that, you realise."

"But what is the matter with Iris!" exclaimed Celia scornfully. "Why on earth can't she stay put? I didn't like to say anything to Mrs. Pole, because she obviously believes that this Keith Anslow is irresistible. But why didn't Iris simply say No when he propositioned her at The Red House? Rushing away, leaving her grandfather and grandmother, when she was supposed to be looking after them! If what he said shocked her, couldn't she tell him to get out?"

"It appears that girls didn't do that to Keith Anslow," said Larry. "It will be rather interesting to meet him."

"I shouldn't be interested to see him at all," said Celia. "He sounds the last word. But, if Iris always runs from him, what's the use of finding him? With him is just where she won't be, surely?"

"If she has run away from him, it means that he came looking for her," said Larry. "And, possibly, since he seems a peculiar chap, he has Burbage still looking for her. It seems to me that Keith's probably got more idea of where to find her than we have. She doesn't go far from her native haunts, and in the old days Keith must have known every one of the friends who helped to cover up for them. I'm quite hopeful that if we find him, he'll give us a lead."

" If he will."

" I don't see any reason why he shouldn't, if he can," said Larry contentedly.

Celia looked at him sharply. Something in his tone gave her the idea that Larry meant to see that Keith did help them, and had not excluded the idea of using force if Keith proved reluctant. But she told herself that she had already been criminally wrong about Larry and his intentions.

The remark changed Celia's mind for her, however. From feeling deep distaste at the idea of having to see Keith Anslow she suddenly became absolutely determined that if Larry interviewed him he should not do it without her.

They took the bus at the bus terminus, and returned to The Red House. When Celia thought about finding Keith she was appalled at the difficulty of the task. They knew nothing about his present life, except that he had been seen in the town one afternoon by Iris Anslow. When Celia pointed this out to Larry, he answered that it would be too much of a coincidence if Keith Anslow happened to be back on a flying visit on the very day when Iris had nerved herself to return after years of avoiding the town.

" But Bill and Flora haven't seen Keith for years," objected Celia. " Surely if he lives here . . ."

" You've seen how much going out they do!" said Larry. " Have you ever been past when Flora was not sitting watching at her window, or Bill pottering about in the garden? I bet they go in to the dentist or the oculist, or for Christmas cards once a year, and that's about all. And, if I know them, they're on their way home again before the rush hour, when anybody who did a job would be out and likely to meet them. Nobody has said yet that Keith Anslow had to retire early because of a weak chest, like Bill. I don't suppose Keith does live in town, actually, but I have a hunch that he hasn't gone far away. We'll have to see."

Celia still considered that it was like looking for a needle in a haystack. On second thoughts, however, the idea did not displease her. She did not care if Larry never found Keith Anslow, just so long as it did not upset him to fail in his search. Her own idea was that Iris would have gone to her baby, wherever he was, but if Larry had not thought of that, she was not anxious to put it into his head. And though she was genuinely sorry for Iris and her miseries, she found it hard to conceal a certain impatience with someone so unbalanced, as she thought, and feeble.

All the evening Larry was in the highest spirits. He sang as he helped Celia to do the supper dishes. He had an idea for tracing Keith, he told her, but he would not tell her what it was, in case it failed. Celia was sure it would fail, and when he kissed her with extra vigour as he set off for the office on Monday morning, she did not turn over and sleep again, as was her usual habit, but lay soberly considering what she could do to cheer him up again on his disappointed return.

She settled for some more painting, and had clothed the bathroom ceiling, an irritating place to tackle, because the floor space underneath was limited, in a pretty translucent green, before the light faded that afternoon. She was stirring the Monday mince—pancakes to follow—when she heard Larry's step coming up the drive. She did not turn for a moment, because she always felt her inside go weak with tenderness whenever she saw Larry's face of dejection, and she knew that at such times she needed rather to be strong. But before she could harden herself he had caught her from behind, and whirled her round, and kissed her vigorously.

"I've got him! I've got his telephone number," he said. "It was easy; as easy as pie."

Celia turned out the gas. This was going to take time, and mince soon hardened.

"How did you do it?" she asked, her face radiant because Larry's was. "Did you ask Burbage?"

"I asked, but not Burbage," said Larry triumphantly and proudly. "No, I simply looked in the local telephone book, and, of course, Anslow wasn't there. But I felt as sure as I could be that he wasn't the man to go very far. So I rang up directory enquiries in the dinner-hour. I didn't let on that I didn't even know which book he would be in. I asked for the neighbouring areas, and waited, and hoped I was getting another girl. But it was all right; at the third try I found him. He was in the book. The address is Hobsford. I thought that as soon as we had had something to eat, we'd go out and ring him up. I could have asked to do it from the office, of course, but the girl listens in, and it's likely to be rather a difficult conversation."

"I see. Well, supper won't take long," said Celia.

They ate at top speed, then Celia put on her coat, and she and Larry went down to the telephone kiosk just opposite the bus terminus. The Anslows were at their own supper, or watching television; their curtains were drawn.

Celia gazed at their lighted window, and thought how strange it was that they had no idea what she and Larry were doing a few yards outside, though it was their business. She stood half in the telephone box, half out, propped against the frame, while Larry was getting the Hobsford number, and doing the talking. She would rather not have listened, yet she wanted to know at once what happened. And, after the first few explanatory questions, Larry's part, too, was chiefly listening. Celia could make nothing of his short answers, and was even doubtful what his expression revealed.

Finally Larry put the phone down, and came out to report.

" It was him all right," he said soberly. " And he does know where Iris is. Burbage traced her for him."

" You were right, then! " exclaimed Celia.

" He says that Iris is living in a room he found her, but he won't say where it is. He says if we want to see her we had better come to his place on Saturday afternoon. Iris is going to be there. We are not to arrive before four o'clock, because he and she have business to discuss. But any time after four will be all right. He has a date then, and will be going out himself."

" Where does he live, exactly?"

" I told you he wouldn't be far away. Hobsford is a village down by the river. He says his place is a cottage called The Willows, and the approach is rather complicated, but anyone will tell us where it is; it's that sort of village. Well, we've done it! Who would have thought it would be so easy! "

" I hope you know what you're going to say to her when you see her," said Celia gently.

Larry looked taken aback.

" I hadn't thought of saying anything in particular," he confessed.

" Oh, darling! " Celia reached up and kissed him. " The great detective! " she said teasingly. " All for the chase."

" I shall say that I simply want to make sure that she is all right," said Larry. " That's natural, isn't it?"

" Yes, but it won't seem natural to her, unless you tell her about Maudie," pointed out Celia.

" I don't know that there would be much sense in that," said Larry uneasily.

Now that the moment was at hand, he seemed embarrassed at the idea of explaining to Iris why he had gone to such trouble to trace her. Celia sympathised with him, but she was amused that the difficulty should only occur to him at this stage.

" We can wait and see how things turn out," she soothed him, and Larry, as if he was a coward, agreed that they would wait and see.

On the Friday evening Larry came home to Celia in triumph. He had bought a car from a friend of his at the office. They would be spared the tedium of buses into town and out again, and a change at Littleworth Green. It was making a holiday of the trip, instead of a duty, and Celia was delighted.

Larry had always loved driving, but he had had to give up his car when he married. He was happy to have his hands on the wheel again. The weather was cold but sunny, and they took a picnic tea with them. They found a quiet place in the woods, and ate very early, then strolled beside the stream. Towards three-thirty Larry began looking at his watch.

" I suppose we mustn't arrive before four, as he particularly told me not to," he said, frowning slightly.

" I wonder what business those two need to discuss?" asked Celia idly.

Larry did not answer. Surprised, Celia looked round at him, and repeated the question.

" What do you suppose?" he asked.

" Oh, Larry, no! " Celia exclaimed.

She was disgusted. And incredulous.

" But Keith's old! " she protested. " He can't be less than forty, surely? It couldn't be, at his age! "

Larry did not speak, so she went on protesting.

" Bill's fifty, at least, and he could be older. And Keith can't be all that much younger," she said. " It was ridiculous enough five or six years ago, but by now they can't have any interest in each other at all, surely? If they have, they ought not to. It can't be! Didn't he give you any idea what they had to talk about?"

" He gave me that idea," said Larry obstinately. " It wasn't anything he said, I admit. It was just the way he said it. I could be wrong, of course."

But he did not think so. Celia dropped the subject, though her mind remained in distasteful contemplation of it during the first minutes of the drive to Hobsford. She could not have expressed how revolting she found it that a man as old as Keith Anslow should consider himself still of an age to make love.

TWENTY-FIVE

THE SIGNPOST said Hobsford, though there were only two cottages to be seen. A little further on, Larry and Celia came to a garage and a public house. Further on still, they made a sharp turn, and found themselves back where they started, beside the two cottages. Celia got out, then, and asked the way. They were sent back to the public house again, and down a lane which had looked to them like a back drive. It had banks on which nettles were growing through old buckets with no bottoms, and damson trees overhanging the hedges.

The Willows, which they reached on the dot of four o'clock, was beside a muddy ill-defined arm of the tiny river. Its name was appropriate, for it was surrounded by willows. They had been cut back and lopped repeatedly, and had grown again, and stood in weird bristling shapes around the rich black earth of a narrow well-cultivated garden. Corrugated iron shelters and water butts, and the like, were dotted all over it. The cool wind could not bend the willow boughs, and made no sound, though there was a noise of water running somewhere nearby.

" He must know a lot about vegetables," said Larry, casting his eye over the garden as they got out of the car. " I suppose that is natural in anyone who was brought up in the lane."

" You would expect a sailor to be tidier," said Celia who was prejudiced.

" I think this probably is tidy," said Larry. " Everything exactly where it is needed, never mind how it looks."

The cottage also had been planned on the same style. It had lean-to's and additions all around a tiny original two up and two down of warm brick and tile. There was a brick path up to the dark green front door. One window, with spotless white curtains, looked down the path, but there seemed to be no one about.

They unlatched the gate, and walked up to the door. Larry lifted the well-polished knocker, and let it fall. Then they waited, rather uncomfortably. Celia did not know what Larry was thinking, but she was waiting to see Keith Anslow with a mixture of dislike, resentment, and curiosity.

The door opened, and he was there.

Celia had sheltered behind Larry, so she had time in which to form her impressions.

She was determined to be contemptuous. She thought at first that it was going to be easy. Keith Anslow looked fifty. He was going bald, from his forehead back across the top of his head, and the wings of strong black hair over his ears only emphasised the sweep of his reddened scalp. Moreover, he was a small man. And rather stout. When he moved to let them into the hall he moved very nimbly, but he reminded Celia of a bouncing ball. She was delighted to be able to find him so unattractive.

This was before he had noticed and spoken to her. The hall inside the front door was so narrow that only one person could stand in it at once, and so Keith led the way immediately into a neat sitting-room overlooking the garden. There Larry turned to introduce Celia, and she and Keith saw each other properly.

Keith smiled, in frank enjoyment of Celia's prettiness. There was nothing offensive in his reaction, and Celia was flattered in spite of herself. And now that she saw his features in animation she had to admit that her first opinion had been too unfavourable. He had bright dark eyes, very lively, which held her own, and seemed to insist on a return of his interest. His colour was high, and reinforced by suntan, his mouth and eyebrows mobile, fascinating to watch. His voice was pleasant.

He was, also, which had its appeal, well turned-out, dressed in a dazzlingly clean shirt and well-creased trousers. Everything about him seemed clean and firm and energetic. Celia began to be not quite so disdainful of his great age.

Keith gave them a seat, and offered them a drink, which they both refused, though he took one himself. There was no sign of Iris, and Celia suddenly became embarrassed again, at the idea that she might at any moment emerge from a bedroom. The house was so tiny that there would be no possibility of concealing where she had been. Celia looked at Keith covertly, while he was talking to Larry about their difficulty in finding the house. She was ashamed of the question that was in her mind, and relieved when she could not guess the answer. Keith looked contented, certainly, as a cat after cream, ready, in spite of his appointment, to lie back in his armchair and talk to them for the rest of the afternoon and evening, but he also seemed wide-awake and vigorous. Celia could come to no conclusion, and with relief gave him and Iris the benefit of the doubt.

Larry was not the type to spend much time on preliminaries.

" Where is Iris?" he asked, after a minute or two.

" She won't be long," answered Keith. Celia did not like the lazy assurance of his tone.

Larry was forced to be patient. He let Keith tell him about the garden. Apparently it was extremely fertile, but drainage was a problem. Keith revealed that he worked in town, in the office of a builder. But his garden was his chief interest; he made it plain that his firm was small and unambitious, and that he did nothing to widen its scope.

There seemed no reason why the conversation should not continue on jobs and hobbies for hours. There was absolutely no sound from upstairs. Celia could feel that Larry was getting restive.

" Does Iris know that we are here?" she asked.

Keith gave her his approving glance.

" I told her that you were coming," he answered. " She shouldn't be long."

" Where is she?" demanded Celia. Let the answer be what it might! If Iris Anslow was in the bedroom, Celia would ask to go up there herself. Anything to force her to appear, before Larry became worked up.

Keith laughed. For some reason the sound jarred. It was frankly reminiscent, rather contemptuous; yet what he said did nothing to explain his tone.

" She's gone for a walk," he said.

" By herself?" asked Larry, in surprise and disapproval.

" Oh, don't worry," said Keith carelessly. " She'll be back when she calms down. We rather got across each other, and she went out to walk it off."

He should have sensed Larry's growing antagonism. Celia could sense it.

"Perhaps we could go to meet her," she suggested.

"No, no, sit down," said Keith, genuinely distressed. "It really isn't worth the trouble. She wouldn't want you to know about the row. It was my fault, I'm afraid. I gave her a shock. But she'll be back all right. She knows you're coming, and that I have arranged to go out."

"What sort of shock?" asked Larry, ignoring the rest of the speech.

Keith began to explain, because Celia was still restless, and he could see that she was on the point of insisting on going out to make a search. His eyes were on her flatteringly as he talked, but she was already, from some instinct, filled again with her previous dislike of him. The hairs were beginning to rise on the back of her neck, as if she had been an animal, and he an enemy.

"We got talking," Keith said. "We had had quite an affectionate reunion, up till that time."

His mouth curled in unashamed amusement, leaving them in no doubt of what his words concealed.

"It's been a long time since we had that sort of chat," he said, still smiling to himself. "I reminded her about the last time, before she left The Red House. I somehow got to talking about the old man."

He paused.

"Iris detested her grandfather, though no one will ever get her to say so," he went on. "Everyone knows he was an old so and so. But no, she pretends that he had his good side. He never showed it to me. I hated the old boy, and the feeling was reciprocated. There wasn't much I could do when I was young, beyond letting his pigs out, and breaking down an apple-tree or two when he wasn't looking, and that was not very rewarding. He always looked as if he would have apoplexy from shouting after me, of course, but it never came to it. I had to wait till I was a grown man and a hero from the wars returning, before I got my own back on him properly."

"How did you do that?" asked Larry, in a neutral tone. He was merely indicating his willingness to hear, for it was plain that Keith intended to tell them, unless he was stopped.

"I'd been amusing myself with Iris one afternoon, when I was home on leave," he said. "The old man was helpless by then, and tucked away in bed, or you may be sure his granddaughter wouldn't have dared have an Anslow in her room, let alone . . ."

He paused deliberately.

"Do go on," said Celia.

She meant to shame him, but she might have known that she couldn't.

"While Iris was tidying up, I had the idea of going to call on the old man," he went on. "I walked into his room, and said Hello to him. He wasn't pleased to see me, but I explained to him that he would have to get used to my being around from then on. I told him that now I was a grown man I was an intimate friend of his granddaughter's. He nearly had a fit."

"It seems I forgot to mention my talk with the old man to Iris. When I spoke about it, this afternoon, she was quite shocked. She got so excited that I suggested she should go for a walk to cool down."

"I suppose you know you killed the old man?" said Larry, getting to his feet. "He had a stroke some time that evening, and died of it."

" Did he? Iris said something like that," answered Keith. " Well, I shouldn't waste any tears. The old chap had been dead for years, actually; they just didn't realise it."

" Which way did she go?" asked Larry, motioning Celia to go ahead of him to the door.

" You're not leaving, are you?" asked Keith, in genuine surprise. " I keep telling you she's got to come back. There's nowhere to go."

" It doesn't sound to me," said Larry, containing his anger with difficulty, " as if she was in a fit state to be wandering around by herself."

" Iris never was," said Keith. " The original little innocent who never grew up. But what do you want with her? What have you come for; I don't think you ever said? Why so concerned?"

" I'm worried about her son," said Larry.

TWENTY-SIX

KEITH'S EYES widened in immense surprise. He stared.

" Iris's son?" he repeated.

" She managed to keep that from you, at any rate," said Larry with grim satisfaction.

" How old is he?" asked Keith, impervious to this.

" Nearly five," said Larry.

" Well, well," Keith said. He added " So Iris had a son! "

His smile broadened. He glanced at Larry swiftly, and then looked down at the floor.

" Did she ever tell you who his father was?" he asked.

" Yes, I know who the father is," said Larry coldly. " We happen to be good friends."

Keith's smile did not go. It turned secret; a smirk.

" Some chaps I've known would have sold their souls for a son," he murmured. " I can't say I ever understood them. But to find you've got one when you hadn't any idea of it—that must really be something! "

" I should have thought that was constantly happening to you," said Celia.

" Don't be saucy," said Keith, smiling with real enjoyment. " I do go to dances in town on Saturdays occasionally; just to see how the old sex appeal is wearing, you know. But don't exaggerate."

" The girls must be thrilled," said Celia. " How did you persuade Mrs. Anslow to come out here?"

Her voice was very hostile, but Keith was still amused.

" Whistled her, and she came to me," he said. " She never could resist me."

" I was under the impression that you went to tremendous trouble to track her from place to place," said Celia. " It sounds more like persecution than a weakness for you, to me."

" Now you are being rude," said Keith genially. " You'd better go and fetch my sister-in-law in. Fancy, my sister-in-law, a mother! What does that make me? We'll all have a drink to it, and thrash the question out. Run along. I'll still be here when you get back."

" Come along, Celia," said Larry.

Keith let them see themselves out of the cottage.

Once they were out; "We'll take her away," Larry said angrily. "We'll bundle her in the car and take her home. If she has luggage here, we'll make her leave it behind. I shall talk plainly to her. She's not going near that chap ever again."

In their haste to get off, they had forgotten to ask again which way Iris had gone. But, as Keith had said, there was only one way. The cottage stood at a dead end. The lane led back towards the village, dull, exposed, mere ground to be covered, quite empty. But a footpath started at the cottage gate, making towards the river bank. The path passed beneath an arch of willows, with an open prospect beyond. It was an invitation, which anyone leaving the cottage would accept instinctively. Larry and Celia turned that way, skirting the muddy patches.

The wind had freshened. The river arm, when they came to it, was ruffled like a piece of watered silk. Celia shivered, and walked closer to Larry. But they had only a few more paces to go. Some previous tenant of the cottage had put a rustic bench upon the bank, beneath the willow trees which marked his boundary. Iris Anslow was sitting upon it.

She had chosen her resting-place well. No one would pass, or if they did, they would see her only from the back, and assume, until dark came, that she was sitting there watching the water. And, after dark, any courting couple finding their seat taken by a stranger, would turn back resentfully without going up to her.

Larry and Celia stepped carefully across the tufted grass, without calling out. They were not surprised that she did not turn round to greet them. And even when Larry spoke, and she did not move, even when they looked into her face, they imagined that after all the agitation she had foolishly fallen asleep.

Then her arm suddenly fell from her lap, with a dull sound. Larry gave an exclamation, and bent closer, feeling her face, trying to see her eyes.

" What is it? Has she fainted?" Celia asked. " Is she dead?"

" I don't know," Larry said. " I don't know anything about such things. Is she breathing; can you tell?"

They held their own breath, and listened, surprised at the difficulty, to the intrusive noise that their own vigorous young hearts, which were nowhere near tired of this life, insisted on making.

" A mirror," said Larry, looking foolishly round as if he might find one on the path.

Celia tumbled her handbag open and thrust her purse mirror at him. Larry's hand trembled as he held it to the sagging mouth.

" I can't tell. I can't tell," he said.

Celia had noticed Iris's purse pushing out of the pocket of her coat. Instinct, she thought, must have made her keep it there, so that when she dared not stop to reclaim her handbag she had always a little money. Celia cautiously withdrew it, feeling absurdly anxious about the liberty she was taking, and looked inside. The first thing she came upon was a chemist's pill bottle.

" What is it?" asked Larry, snatching. He took it from Celia's hand, and held it so that they could read the label.

There was the printed name and address of a Birmingham chemist. And above it, in ink, almost obliterated,

The Rev. E. E. L. Jones,

and above that again, " The capsules, one to be taken twice

daily." And across the whole label someone had written in almost indecipherable pencil, " Never more than four."

The bottle was quite empty. Larry tilted it to make sure, knowing that it was empty.

" The clergyman, the one she was housekeeper to," said Celia.

" God knows what was prescribed for him," said Larry in a rage. " But, whatever it was, there was probably plenty left over, and she has taken the lot."

" Is she dead?" asked Celia.

" She could be. Yet it can't have been long. We must do something quick," said Larry.

" Wake her," suggested Celia. " And walk her about."

" I think it's too late for that. Yet it will be an hour before we can get her to hospital," said Larry.

They spoke to her, patted her face, rubbed her hands, Larry wheedled her.

" Iris! " he said. " Wake up. It's Larry. I'll look after you, Iris, if you'll only get well. Wake up, speak to me, Iris. Wake up."

It was useless. After a minute or two they acknowledged it.

" We've wasted time," said Larry angrily. " And every minute matters. We've got to go and ring up. Or would it be better to drive straight away with her? I don't know what is the best thing to do."

It was strange to hear him at a loss. Celia instantly became firm and decisive.

" We can do both," she said. " You take her, while I ring up from the cottage to give warning."

" They won't know what to do. The first thing they need to know is what she has taken," Larry said.

" I'll ring up the chemist," said Celia. "If he is closed, I'll ask the telephone exchange for the address of the Reverend E. E. L. Jones. It may still be in the book. Someone there may know his doctor or his sister. I could be lucky; you never know. Then I can get the information to you."

" I'll never carry her to the car," Larry said. " She's a dead weight."

He winced at what he had said.

" Keith is there. He must help you," Celia said. " Hurry, in case he takes it into his head to go out, after all."

They ran to the cottage, feeling as if they were abandoning the woman under the willows, but hoping that by leaving her they were helping her. They rushed up the path to the cottage door, and found Keith standing on the step, alerted by the banging of the gate.

" You must come and help Larry," cried Celia. " Iris has poisoned herself, and we have to get her to hospital."

For a second Keith Anslow stood stock-still.

" Done it, after all, has she?" he exclaimed.

It was then, after so much idle thought of it, that Celia looked for the first time on the true face of murder. And murder was not violent, she saw, nor shame-faced, not shrieking, nor shrinking from what it had done. Murder had hooded eyes, veiled to conceal their mirthful satisfaction, a small mouth primming to a secret smile. Celia stood gazing, transfixed.

Then the eyes opened, the mouth broadened into a normal expression, Keith Anslow moved out of the doorway, and spoke again.

" Where is she? I'd better give you a hand, I suppose," he said competently.

TWENTY-SEVEN

THE CHIEF witness at the inquest was not Larry, nor Keith Anslow, nor Bill, but a Dr. Severall. Iris had lingered in a coma for a week, giving ample time for the police to contact him. And he rewarded their effort. He spoke of Iris's selfless devotion during the last illness of the Reverend Ellis Jones, of her days and nights of nursing, unsparing of time and patience. It was the devotion of a daughter, more than many a real daughter showed, he said, glancing under his pepper and salt eyebrows at the Reverend Ellis Jones's black-clad affronted daughter. He spoke in a neutral voice of that daughter's request to Iris to leave at the end of a week, enforced because she felt there was something unhealthy in the hired help's grief at the old man's death. He acknowledged and identified the pills Iris had taken.

While he spoke, and Celia's eyes were fixed on him, marvelling at human feeling from such a dried-up-looking little man, a word to explain Iris's behaviour to her employer was trying to form itself on her lips.

" Expiation! " she murmured at last. " She was trying to atone for being such a bad girl to her grandfather."

Larry bent to ask what Celia had said. She shook her head at him to warn him to be silent, for now they were coming to the end of the story as the police saw it—Iris's pilgrimage to her old home to look up her relations, her old friends. Keith testified that she had invited herself to his cottage, after they had not seen each other for years. She had arrived depressed, but he had imagined that she had cheered up by the time she left him to go for a walk by the river while he changed for his date.

The sympathies of those listening were with him. It was a dirty trick, they considered, to look a man up after so many years simply for the purpose of committing suicide on his doorstep.

It was true, and it was false. Afterwards Celia and the Bill Anslows stood around for a moment, at a loss, avoiding each other's eyes, guarding their words, unable to believe that it was all over. Then they scattered like sparrows before a cat as Keith Anslow came out, and seemed about to approach them. He had a black hat, and a black tie, and a solemn look on his handsome face, but there was exuberance in every movement, and in the spring of him.

Nothing came out at the inquest about Iris's child, or his whereabouts. At Bill's request, urged on by Larry in the wings, a question was put by the police to Iris's mother in hospital, but they reported her too senile to understand: her doctor would not commit himself to whether or not this was pretence on her part. But on this question, to Celia's relief, Larry seemed now prepared to accept defeat.

The flatness of the first days after the inquest was strange. Celia's thoughts revolved Iris's fate constantly, turning it up again and again when she had consciously pushed it down. She felt physically obstructed because Larry hated to discuss it. She was a little relieved by the discovery that she had at last become one of the village. They no longer stared in the shops; they broke off serving to greet her, and enquired after her health as greedily as if she had been pregnant. And now, too, Celia had friends in the lane; Flora and Bill.

Flora did not leave the house, except on the morning when Bill surreptitiously made an honest woman of her. Celia used to look in on her way to the shops, and again as she returned, with whatever little commission Flora had found for her. They talked a lot about Iris in youth, but never about her end.

Iris had been buried in the same churchyard as the Reverend Ellis Jones. It was a bus journey away, but Flora, showing a hardness which astonished Celia, had refused to have her buried anywhere locally. Neither she nor Bill visited the grave.

Celia felt guilty about this. It happened that Larry was working overtime almost every evening. There was a bus out to Iris's village on Thursday afternoons. Celia took it one day after Christmas, arranging to meet Larry in town on her return, and come home with him, since the bus time fitted.

The church of St. Chad was very old. Its squat tower was crouched in the graveyard, the rough lawn on the south side mounded to nearly window level.

" It's bones that have brought the ground up to that height," Celia reminded herself, as she opened the gate, and walked up the moss-grown path. " But they all look very cosy," she said aloud, as she stared at the comfortably-leaning gossiping old grave-stones.

Iris had been buried on the less populated north side, on a slope open to the keen spring wind. Celia had come provided with a cheap vase and some anemones. She set them on the raw earth. She had had to identify the grave by counting; there could be no stone erected till the ground had settled, Larry said.

Celia felt she should pray, but the right words eluded her. She turned away, and saw Keith Anslow walking between the grave plots towards her.

" They say murderers do haunt the graves of their victims! " she exclaimed. But, of course, no one could actually call Keith a murderer. She would have avoided him if she could, but it was not possible. They were alone in the deserted churchyard, and he had come upon her before she noticed him.

Keith was surprised to meet Celia, and curious, and pleased, but not in the least abashed.

" Fancy seeing you here! " he exclaimed.

" Fancy seeing you! " Celia retorted, but he did not take her bitter meaning.

" I have Thursday afternoons off; didn't I ever tell you?" he said. " I meant to come before; but the weather has been too wet for bedding-out."

Celia saw that he had a bag with him. He bent and took out a trowel, and blundles of newspaper-wrapped plants. She noticed, when he stooped, the bald patch on his head.

" You are not going to plant Iris's grave?" she exclaimed, her sense of what was fitting completely outraged.

" They'll be all right. They're good strong plants. I grew them myself, so I know," Keith returned, misunderstanding her. " They're primroses, and those in my own garden are flowering now, when the birds will let them alone. I shouldn't think the sparrows would tear the buds off here."

" But why are *you* doing it?" Celia demanded.

Keith could not mistake her meaning this time.

" Oh, well," he replied, smiling. " It's a long way for the other two to come. And they're not up to it. I didn't think they would want the trouble, although, of course, as they got Iris's money . . ."

The Reverend Ellis Jones had bequeathed fifty pounds to his housekeeper, Iris Anslow, if she was still in his service at the time of his death. The legacy would go to Bill, her husband, although he had been spending his life with another woman.

Keith spoke of Bill's inheritance with keen amusement. He was not envious, Celia discovered. He talked of his brother with unshakeable contempt, but he did not grudge Bill money. Bill needed all the luck he could get, he indicated. He was soft inside. Whereas he, Keith, knew how to look after himself. He had everything he wanted, and a reserve for a rainy day, and did not need any old dotard's money.

He spoke genially even of the old dotard. His satisfaction was entire. Celia was sure that he had no sense of guilt. When he thought of Iris it was probably with scornful amusement that she had not been able to cope. He had brought his plants because he was a keen gardener, and did not bear poor little Iris a grudge.

Celia said she would go and stand at the bus stop. She had at least half an hour to wait for her bus, but she had not expected to be done so soon.

" If you'll wait a few minutes, while I put these in, I'll run you to town. I've got my car here," said Keith.

He was friendly, pleased to be of service, in no way self-conscious.

Celia was glad to be able to inform him that it would not suit her to get to town early, because she was meeting Larry.

" And he'll be looking forward to seeing you waiting there as he comes out," nodded Keith. " I only hope he appreciates you."

" I think he does," said Celia. She could not help a smile.

Keith smiled, too, apparently in pure pleasure at the idea of young love.

" Let me know if he doesn't, and I'll come and bash him," he offered facetiously. " After all, we've got a link now, haven't we?"

His secret smirk showed for a moment. Celia kept silent.

" You're very glum. Yet you've got a sweet little smile, did you know?" said Keith unexpectedly. " You remind me of my mother, as a matter of fact. She must have been a dainty little thing, like you, when she was young, though by the time we boys were old enough to notice her looks something had knocked the stuffing out of her. But when the money was coming in, and she wasn't worried, she had a way of smiling with her eyes that could wheedle anything out of anyone."

" I'm cold. I'll go and wait in the church," said Celia abruptly. She was shaken by the compliment, because it was obviously made without any ulterior motive.

" The door's usually locked," Keith said. But he bent to his work, and did not try to detain her.

The church was locked. Celia stood within the porch, and read the notices, and shivered. She resented it when Keith came along again, rosy from the wind and his stooping, glowing with health and cheerful.

" You're perished," he said, concern in his voice. " You'll get your death, if you aren't careful. Come back to the cottage with me, and I'll brew you a cup of tea. With a dash of good stuff in it. Then you can catch your bus."

" No, thank you," said Celia.

Keith looked at her, slightly surprised, seeing not much significance in her avoidance of him, but just enough to be worth scrutinising.

" What's the matter?" he asked. " Are you thinking that I'm a bachelor? But that doesn't signify. None of the old busybodies in Hobsford could see anything wrong in my giving you a cup of tea. Not that they'll know; I'm not over-looked."

" I'd rather not, thank you," said Celia.

" Is it Larry you're afraid of? Is he the jealous type? But he wouldn't be jealous of me," Keith rallied her.

" Of course not," said Celia. She would have liked to say spitefully, " You're much too old," but something—could it be a regard for the truth? restrained her.

" Suit yourself," said Keith. " Shall I see you here next week?"

" No," said Celia.

TWENTY-EIGHT

THE NEXT Thursday Celia took the bus to St. Chad's again. She told herself that Keith would probably not be there.

She told herself that, if he was, she had a right to study him, to try to find a way to shake his complacency, to make him admit the dreadful thing he had done to Iris. But the truth was that Larry had not seemed delighted to see her outside the office, as Keith had predicted. Larry explained crossly that, as it happened, he had been able to finish at the usual time, and so had been kept twiddling his thumbs waiting for her, when he was aching to get home because he felt a cold developing.

Larry with a feverish cold was a revelation to Celia. He would take no remedies, yet he never ceased to complain. He hung about the house, refusing to go to bed, shuddering whenever she opened a door, coughing, sneezing, for four interminable days. Celia, who had been brought up to be spartan about illness, could not help despising him. That was really why she went back to St. Chad's without arranging to meet Larry on her return through the town.

She had been in the churchyard only a few minutes when Keith joined her, as before. His surprise and pleasure was spontaneous, and, in spite of Celia's distrust of him, very warming.

Nothing happened. Celia refused once more to go back with Keith to his cottage. But she did not protest when he walked with her to the bus stop and stood chatting until she got on; nor at his confident, " See you next week, then," as she was borne away.

Celia told Larry that evening where she had been. He seemed pleased, though surprised. She said that she would be visiting the churchyard again, and he was grateful. He was still preoccupied with the rush of work which might force him to do overtime for months. When Celia saw that Larry had not taken in that she was going to St. Chad's regularly, she did not bring up the subject again. When he came in on Thursday evening she did not remind him that she, too, had been out.

Deep in her heart she knew well enough that she would end by visiting Keith's cottage. It only needed the excuse of a bus breaking down, or bad weather. If nothing happened to the bus, how could the weather not be bad eventually, in an outrageously wild and windy month? Celia had only to wait; and sure enough, she got off the bus one afternoon in a vicious downpour, to find Keith standing with an umbrella and spare mackintosh, ready to rush her across the flooded road to his car.

The cottage was cosy. Keith had a huge coal fire roaring up the chimney. He gave Celia a spotlessly clean towel to rub her wet legs with, showed her where to wash and dry her stockings. He made her tea, without fuss, but giving her the feeling that he cared for her comfort. When they settled down to wait out the storm he talked to amuse her. His year in Australia and his time at sea had given him plenty to say. And he talked to interest Celia, not to show himself in a good light to her, nor to feed her nostalgia.

Without anything being said, Celia made no attempt to catch the return bus. She left her flowers with Keith, and he ran her into town, as he had proposed to do the first time they met.

The next Thursday, Keith was once more waiting for her. It was a fine day. They walked to the churchyard with Celia's flowers, and then went straight back to the cottage for tea. Keith had baked a cake, an attention which touched Celia.

The afternoon put life into her. In spite of what she

knew about Keith she could only discover one fault in him. He hated to be laughed at. In that he reminded Celia irresistibly of a tom-cat her family had owned. This cat had once skidded on the polished floor in front of a roomful of people, who had burst out laughing. The cat had gone away and hidden under a bed, and the next day he was still sulking and refusing to come and be petted. Keith was like that. He talked amusingly against himself, but a single hint that Celia might be thinking him absurd stiffened him in badly concealed annoyance.

But it only happened once; Celia withdrew instantly.

Celia was not in the least attracted to Keith. She knew it, and felt safe. But to make sure that the undoubted fascination he had for her was not sexual, she used to force him to talk about Iris.

Keith always protested. She always insisted. And so he told her a great deal about life in the lane and at The Red House, in the old days. But it aways came back to the same thing; Iris Belmont had thought herself a cut above him. When Keith first attempted to make up to her, for a joke, she had put him off. Even after they had kissed, when he sat down beside her on the bus she had pretended she did not know him. He had vowed then to take her down a peg. And he had done it.

Not all Iris's grovelling afterwards, when she took the initiative to arrange their meetings in the loft, to miss classes, to deceive her grandparents, had expiated her crime. Keith had never forgotten; even now, when she was dead, he did not forgive.

Celia noted all this, sitting weekly in the armchair opposite him, looking at his flushed face, and cataloguing his errors with pride. She felt clear-sighted, very much a judge.

It blinded her to any danger. How could she, who saw all his weakness, show any to him herself?

It happened quite suddenly. Keith always insisted on waiting on Celia. He came across to pick up her empty cup. Celia had an irresistible urge to touch his cheek.

She felt him stiffen, and for a fraction of time was apprehensive. But Keith turned up to her a face alight with understanding.

" It's a pity about Larry," he said.

" Why?" asked Celia. She was astonished to hear her voice sound petulant.

" I wouldn't want to upset Larry," Keith said.

" Why not?"

" It doesn't seem quite the thing, does it?" Keith said in a regretful voice.

" I didn't know you were so fond of him," retorted Celia.

" No, but it's rather a special thing, isn't it?" said Keith. " I rather draw the line . . . But, after all, why should I bother about him? Come here, my sweet—we'll show him a thing or two."

He drew Celia up to him, and began to kiss her.

The moment Keith's mouth touched hers, Celia started back. She was astounded at the revulsion she felt because his lips were not Larry's. She pulled away with all her strength, but it was a minute before Keith would let her go.

Keith was as angry as might have been expected.

" What are you playing at?" he asked, trying to drag her to him again. " You don't think you can lead me on, and then give me the brush off like this, do you? Come on, you know you really want it. Never mind about Larry: he isn't going to find out, and what he doesn't know about won't hurt him."

He seized Celia again. Once again she struggled free. She saw with alarm that Keith was not going to give up. She cursed herself for getting into this position; and panicked.

"Larry *is* going to know," she said. "I shall tell him. I tell him everything."

Keith merely smiled.

"Do you tell him about this?" he asked, indicating the cottage, the tea spread out. "I bet you haven't."

"Of course I have," cried Celia. "I tell him everything. He knows I only come for him, because he wants to hear about Iris."

"Hear about Iris?" repeated Keith. "What sort of tale is that?"

Celia had made a slight impression. He was listening, instead of speaking at random while he reached out for her again.

"He wants to know about Iris, because she was his foster-sister," said Celia, retreating across the hearth. "I tell him all you say. That's all I come for."

"That's a tale," retorted Keith. "We both know what you come for. We've always known."

"It's not. It never was that. You're too old," said Celia desperately.

"I'm not so old that I couldn't teach Larry a thing or two," said Keith.

"You are. I laugh at you. Larry laughs at you, too, because you don't know I think you're too old," Celia said.

She saw then that Murder had a second face. It advanced on her, fixed in a snarl, stiff, bestial, recking nothing. She screamed, and the grin widened in anticipation without losing its cruelty.

Celia snatched at the only weapon, the poker.

"Keep off," she said, feebly brandishing it. "If you come near me, I'll kill you."

Keith halted; and smiled.

"I could take that off you as easily as taking candy off a kid," he said.

"Then I'll set the whole house on fire," threatened Celia.

She turned in a flash, and pushed the poker into the fire, scraping out flaming coals, frantically digging. They fell to the rug, and set up an immediate sickening stench and thin smoke.

"Stop that," Keith said, gripping her wrist. At once she caught up a sheet of newspaper, set it on fire, and dropped it, flaming, at Keith's feet.

Murder had its priorities, Celia found. Its own skin came first. With a muttered curse Keith stamped out the flames which were licking round his shoes. Celia took her opportunity, and darted out of the house.

She fled down the lane, knowing that Keith could catch her if he chose to get out his car. But she was lucky. When she had covered a hundred yards from the cottage she overtook an old woman who was walking towards the bus stop. Celia, breathless, slowed to a walk, and offered to carry her basket.

The old woman suspiciously refused. But she could not forbid Celia to walk beside her. A minute later the car roared past them, turned and backed further up the lane, and then passed them again, so close that it almost grazed them. The old woman forgot her hostility as she turned to gaze

F

after Keith, and tell Celia what she thought of road-hogs. Celia did not admit any connection, and they went and waited together, undisturbed by Keith, for the bus.

TWENTY-NINE

THE WHOLE of the way home Celia's determination to tell Larry everything was fixed and unshakeable. She waited in a frenzy of self-hatred, and the moment he came through the back door she flew at him, burying her face against him.

" Here, what is it?" he exclaimed in concern.

Celia raised her face.

" Oh, Larry, I'm so upset! " she began.

" I'm sorry," he said. " What about?"

His voice was affectionate, but, above Celia's head, he was looking round for the peg on the wall. She slid out of his arms, and helped him take off and hang up his heavy coat. He turned to her again.

"What's gone wrong, then?" he asked kindly.

" Nothing," Celia replied. " I get tired of waiting for you. It suddenly came over me."

" Perhaps you should get out more?" suggested Larry.

Celia agreed that she should and would. It was fairly easy to make Larry forget her panic. She knew now that she would never tell him about Keith and herself.

Confession would have been easier. Unrelieved, she felt like a scarlet woman. She imagined, as she went to do her shopping, that all the village was watching her, guessing what had happened, condemning. Next day she turned in the opposite direction.

The lane led uphill and down dale to a different sub-merged village, with a quite different bus route to town, which was why, as far as Celia's neighbours were concerned, it might as well have been in Scotland or Wales. Celia could rely on meeting no one she knew there.

There was only one shop. Mrs. Jones, who owned it, was brisk the first time Celia entered. The second time, she smiled, and made an amiable remark. For some reason no one else came in to be served, which suited Celia well enough. But, on the third occasion, the doorbell jangled, and the old woman Celia had taken refuge with, when she was escaping from Keith Anslow, walked in.

Celia gave her a startled look, and an uncertain smile. Mrs. Jones nodded, and said,

" Good morning, Mrs. Ryder."

Celia's smile was ignored, but a sort of snort acknowledged the shopkeeper's greeting.

Mrs. Ryder had a sour square face, with mouth bent down into lines of suspicion. She was between sixty and seventy. To Celia she seemed to typify all the village people who sensed she was a guilty woman. Embarrassed, she turned back to the counter, and concentrated on getting served. She would have to leave without the chat with Mrs. Jones she might have hoped for on that day.

Celia placed her purchases in her bag, paid, and turned to go out. In doing so she stepped back into the old lady, who had moved to stand right behind her. Celia apologised, but was met with a look so hostile that the words tailed off. She fled from the shop without finishing what she was saying. And just outside the door she fell over a push-chair.

It was drawn up right in the doorway, and held a small child. Celia was aware, before she looked at him, that something had dropped from his hand. Probably in brushing against him she had made him let go of his toy. She stooped to pick it up, and handed it anxiously back. Her eyes were on the child's face. Would he howl, and bring that dreadful old crone down upon her?

The child took the toy from her, without a word and without a smile. He had large blue eyes, sombre, unfriendly, and a face stained with the remains of many meals. His hair-cut looked as if it had been done round a pudding basin, and his clothes were shabby. It was a long time since Celia had seen a child who was not clean and well-kept, and with an impulse of pity she stayed to try to make him smile at her. But his eyes remained unwinking, his face solemn. In desperation Celia tried calling his attention to his toy.

" Pretty! " she said encouragingly, and looked more closely to see what she was praising.

It had once been a fluffy pale-blue rabbit. It was still recognisably a rabbit, though grey and smeared with dirt. She stared. The child stared. Then Celia turned and walked rapidly away.

She was half-way towards home before she realised it. She looked up in surprise, and saw the hollybush which marked the bend in the lane beyond The Red House. She had no idea how she had come there.

Celia was a sensible girl. She told herself that there were other blue rabbits, hundreds of thousands of them, clutched by children in push-chairs all over the world. There was no reason why this one should have anything to do with Larry. But Celia knew. The rabbit was the one Larry had bought in Majorca, and the baby was Iris's son.

When people said that a man ought to marry a girl, with malice in their hearts, they usually meant that he had got her into trouble. Was that what the anonymous letter-writer had meant about Larry, after all? That Larry was the father of a baby, ought to have been marrying the mother, instead of Celia? But Larry would never do such a thing!

Celia found her way to her door. The drive from the gate was clear of weeds, the beds by the outbuildings neat and tidily edged. Inside, the house was light and luminous. The Red House was a changed place, and the inspiration, the vision behind it, was Larry's. Celia took comfort from the evidence of his love of rightness and order. He would never do something so undisciplined and untidy as to seduce a girl he had looked on as a sister, who already had a husband.

The evidence of Celia's eyes assured her of that, while instinct was warning her that if the rabbit had been innocently given away, Larry would have told her about it. And when Celia tried to think what other friendship, what complication, could account for the secrecy, she was brought up short. Larry had been in search of a baby. There could not be two missing babies in his life. It was Iris's baby he had been searching for, Iris's baby he had given the blue rabbit to, and Iris whom the anonymous letter-writer claimed he ought to have made his wife.

Celia went into the house, and up to her bedroom. Mechanically she took off her coat, hung it in the wardrobe, closed the door. Then for a moment she laid her aching forehead against the coldness of the long mirror. All the training of her happy childhood, her happy family life, urged her to be open with Larry. If she suspected that he had an illegitimate child, living in the next village, she must ask him outright, give him a chance to deny, explain, defend himself. But another part of her mind warned her that Larry had not had a free and friendly family life. He had been an only child, with a managing and headstrong mother. Frank discussion might not seem natural to him. ' But I must know,' said the level-headed part of Celia, and from the depths a deeper instinct replied, ' Ah, but I don't want to know.'

The debate gave her a headache, much worse than what had gone before, but at least she made up her mind. She would ask Larry tonight, as soon as he came in, what he had done with the blue rabbit. That would give him a chance to explain, if he wanted to take it.

THIRTY

IT WAS always six o'clock before Larry arrived, and often much later. Celia went into the pantry, to get their own apples, to make a pie. Larry loved apple pie. If it was treacherous to give him a favourite dish when she planned to question him, then Celia was treacherous; she wanted Larry to enjoy his supper, at least.

Five minutes later, as she stood at her pastry-board, the door opened. The next moment Larry had laid his fingers over her eyes and said laughingly,

" Guess who?"

Celia was filled with a rush of love and tenderness. Larry found it hard to be playful. He was naturally passionate, and could be tender, but little jokes, family teasing, did not come easy to him. He was learning from her. She caught has hand to her cheek in a loving gesture, and said,

" Why are you so early? I didn't hear you. Are you home to stay?"

" I was out inspecting a desirable residence," said Larry, kissing her, and then picking up an apple. " The boss said it wouldn't be worth while going back to the office, so here I am. Don't you want me? Shall I go back again?"

" You've done yourself out of an apple pie," said Celia, laughing back at him. " It will have to be stewed apples instead. And we'll have cold meat, and get a lovely long evening for once."

And no questions, she told herself. Larry loved her, and she loved him, whatever he had done. She would leave well enough alone.

She laughed and chattered all evening. But towards eleven, as they were sitting relaxed, with the curtains drawn, Larry said quietly,

" Don't you feel well?"

Celia was taken by surprise, but she rallied. " Of course. Why do you ask? Don't I look it?" she said brightly.

" Then, are you worried about something?" he asked.

" Of course not," she answered sharply.

She never snapped at him. Larry looked startled. Then he withdrew into silence. Celia's heart ached for him, but what could she say? She got up to make a bedtime drink, leaving Larry in the sitting-room.

Just as the milk was boiling he came into the kitchen. She poured it into the cups, and motioned to him to take the tray. But instead he turned her into his arms, and laid her head against him.

" Tell me what it is," he said, in his most loving voice.

Before, when Larry had used that voice, Celia was convinced that he could and would defend her against the whole world, against poverty, atom bombs, sickness, even death. It worked on her now.

" I was wondering what you did with that toy rabbit you bought in Majorca," she said into his shoulder.

With horror she felt Larry stiffen against her. The next moment, realising that he had betrayed himself, he put her away from him. " I didn't know you knew about it," he said.

It was not an answer. Celia noted it with anguish.

" I saw it in your case," she said briefly, and looked questioningly at him again.

" It was for the child of someone I know," said Larry.

There was a silence.

" Iris's?" asked Celia at last. But she knew the answer.

" Yes," Larry said.

Celia waited, but Larry seemed to be going to say nothing more. She looked down and saw the tray.

" We'd better have our drink," she said with relief, and picked up the tray.

" Let me," said Larry, starting forward.

" No," said Celia. She spoke with more force than was necessary, clutching the tray dangerously and absurdly to her. She was refusing him more than the privilege of carrying it, and they both knew it. Larry's eyes dropped before hers.

Embarrassed, she turned away from him, and made her way through the door, and into the sitting-room. She put the tray on the low table between their chairs, drew it into a convenient position, all the old gestures, empty now, but repeated automatically. Larry came and sat down, took his cup. He had one sip of coffee.

Then he put his cup violently down, slopping the liquid into the saucer.

" I couldn't do a thing while I was alone," he said. " But when we got married, and we had our own house . . . I kept thinking that we might have him here. Only Iris had absolutely refused to tell me where he was."

" No," said Celia. She rose to her feet with the force of her inner revolt. She wanted children, longed for them, but they were to be hers and Larry's. And they were to come first. That their first child should be adopted, illegitimate, taking the place and the honour of their own first-born! No, never. There was a churning in her inside as if her womb itself was protesting.

" I suppose you would feel like that," said Larry humbly.

" I do feel like that," said Celia angrily. It hurt her that Larry should be humble. She had always admired him for his glorious certainty, because he knew what had to be done, and did it without hesitation or regrets.

"What made you think of it tonight?" asked Larry abruptly.

" I had a letter," said Celia.

" A letter? When?" He was startled. He imagined it had arrived that day.

" I found it in the car when we set off on our honeymoon," Celia told him. She saw that he was profoundly shocked, and she rejoiced in it.

" Why didn't you tell me?" he asked in a mortified voice.

" I didn't want to," she answered cruelly.

There was no reply to this. Larry said nothing. Celia sat down on the arm of her chair and coldly watched him.

" Who was the letter from?" he asked at last.

" I don't know. It wasn't signed. Does it matter?"

" It would be Iris's mother, I expect," said Larry, in the same defeated voice. " I was terrified that she meant to cause trouble in church."

It was Celia's turn to feel shocked. " Was that what was the matter with you?" she asked.

" Yes, I was afraid she had come just to make a scene."

And Celia had wasted pity on him, trying to protect him from Steve's jokes, imagining he had a bad attack of nerves!

" I think she started to say something," said Larry. " But she must have had a glimmer of sense, and thought better of it. Fortunately mother was not there—they would have set each other off. Mother was afraid to come, she said, in case she let out something she shouldn't, about Iris."

In the icy calm which had descended upon her Celia felt no desire to ask further questions. Larry volunteered no more explanations. They finished their coffee, and then, with only the routine conversation about doors and windows, went up the stairs to bed. They did not lie for a little while, to discuss the events of the day, as their habit was, but turned to sleep with a curt Goodnight. Some time before dawn Celia roused, and saw that she had put her arm across Larry's shoulder as usual. She left it there, but he did not wake, and she finally fell asleep again herself.

THIRTY-ONE

THEY HAD a miserable week-end, though on the face of it everything was normal. They worked in the garden, made a plan for a back porch, and drove into town for a film and supper afterwards. But the joy had gone out of life, and for once Celia saw Larry drive off on the Monday morning with real relief.

She spent the morning in washing. She left everything billowing on the line, and went up to change. Afterwards she saw that nothing was ready for ironing. She decided to go down to the shop.

Mrs. Jones received her with her usual reserved smile. Celia bought groceries, some of which she didn't want, and on impulse added a bright packet of jelly babies. She couldn't have told anyone what she had bought it for, but as soon as she left the shop she knew. She was going to have another look at Larry's son. Bad taste perhaps, unwelcome to the woman the baby lived with, but she was under a compulsion.

She had no idea where Mrs. Ryder's house was, and was stumped momentarily by the difficulty of finding out. Celia was perplexed, but not to be put off. And presently her problem solved itself, for a familiar little red van came in sight round the bend of the street. The mail van with the parcel post. She spoke to the driver, and after a moment's cogitation he directed her to a turning where she could just see a block of cottages.

Celia walked towards them, moving jauntily as if she knew where she was going, in case curious eyes were watching her. But when she rounded the bend she relaxed, for the two cottages were quite isolated. In the near one there was washing blowing, but not so much as a cat stirring. In the further one, which was Mrs. Ryder's, no washing, but no movement, either.

Celia marched up to the front door, and pressed the bell. She heard nothing, so tried again, keeping her finger on it. Nothing stirred. Celia seized the dingy knocker, and beat a tattoo. Still nothing happened.

She stood biting her lip uncertainly, then started resolutely towards the back of the house. Before she could get there a woman came through the hedge which divided the two gardens, and confronted her.

" Were you wanting something?" she asked.

It was a young woman, aggressively clean, slightly wary, like everyone here.

" I wanted to see Mrs. Ryder," said Celia.

" She's out," said the young woman. " I'm Mrs. Wicken from next door. Can I give her a message?"

" Will Mrs. Ryder be long?" countered Celia.

" Long enough," said the woman with a touch of rough irony. " She's taken the bus into town. She does that on Monday afternoons. She usually goes to the pictures with a friend before she comes back."

" I'll come again," said Celia uncomfortably. She began to walk back down the path, and then remembered the sweets.

"I bought these for the little boy," she said awkwardly. "Perhaps you could give them to him when you see him?"

"You can give them to him yourself," said Mrs. Wicken, in a voice which was suddenly so rude that Celia was startled. She went red, and was in two minds whether to protest, but without waiting for her reaction the woman was leading the way round to the back of the cottage. After a second's hesitation, Celia followed her.

The back garden was a desolation of weeds, and rubbish worse than weeds, old buckets without bottoms, rotted planks, broken cups, the debris of years. The drain smelt, and so did the house, when Mrs. Wicken, without ceremony, pushed open the back door. It led straight into a largish room which was both scullery and kitchen. It was a dreary place, dim, and smelling of rank floor-cloths, mice, mustiness, stale tea-leaves and cabbage-water. It was cluttered with battered enamel bowls, rags, bursting cushions, piles of newspapers, baskets of sprouting potatoes. But the dreariness was on the whole due more to age and clutter than to dirt. There was a table in the middle of the room covered with the salt and pepper, the sugar-bowl and tea-caddy, the sauce-bottle, the dirty plates, of innumerable meals. It was obviously never cleared, though a corner of the table-cloth might sometimes be pushed aside to give room to prepare vegetables or write a letter.

At first, taking in the evidence of disorganised living, Celia did not see the boy. Then Mrs. Wicken directed her attention with an elbow in her side.

He was sitting on the rag rug in front of the black empty hearth. An old coat had apparently been thrown round him, but he had thrown it off. He had the blue rabbit in his mouth, and was sucking it. He turned his head when the women spoke, but did not make a sound.

" What's his name?" asked Celia diffidently.

Mrs. Wicken gave her a curious look.

" Johnny," she said.

" I've brought some sweets for you, Johnny," said Celia.

Johnny removed his rabbit to stare at her, but still did not speak. His solemn blue eyes were set in a grubby face. Celia tried to find a hint of Larry, but failed. She held out the packet, but Johnny did not get up.

" Here, I'll give him one," said Mrs. Wicken, with pitying impatience. She seized the packet, forced it open, grumbling at the toughness of the bag as she did so, then fell on her knees and offered the child a jelly baby. He took it cautiously, solemnly examined it, then put it into his mouth and smiled. Celia was relieved to watch something so normal. For a dreadful moment she had thought Larry's son was an idiot.

Mrs. Wicken placed the bag on the rug. " There you are, Johnny-boy," she said. " Help yourself. The kind lady's brought them all for you. And don't howl for me if you knock them away and can't reach them, for I've got to go back to work."

" Can't he stand?" asked Celia diffidently. She was not really very well-up in child-care, but Larry's son should have been long since old enough to walk.

" He can stand if he's let," said Mrs. Wicken angrily. Her sudden bursts of rudeness were quite inexplicable to Celia, and she looked at her with quick resentment, but Mrs. Wicken was unabashed.

" Can't you see that he's tied?" she said roughly.

Celia gave an exclamation of horror. She knelt down

impulsively, and saw that it was true. The child was tied, by a short length of picture cord round his waist to a ring in the floorboards. The horrible thing was that the ring had obviously been knocked in there specially to tie down a small boy.

Celia began to struggle with the cord. " Can't you let him loose?" she asked Mrs. Wicken reproachfully.

" Are you the welfare?" demanded Mrs. Wicken.

" No."

" Then you'd better leave him alone," said Mrs. Wicken.

" Why?" Celia asked.

" Of course I could let him loose! " burst out Mrs. Wicken. " But it's more than my life's worth. I did do it once, and I never heard the last of it from the old lady. She won't let me mind him even when I offer, but of course I can't suggest it often—I'm a waitress part-time, at a road-house, and I work all sorts of odd hours. And my husband says not to get across the old lady. We have to live next door to her, and she's the sort who can turn very nasty if you cross her, very spiteful indeed. I wouldn't let that bother me, though, if I wasn't out most of the time myself. But something ought to be done. At first she only tied him up when she had to go out in bad weather and couldn't take him, but it's got to be that she does it every time she wants a nap, or when she goes to the churchyard, or into town, like now. And it's my belief he lives on what she does, just strong tea and bread and butter. It isn't right. He's a forward little chap, but she's turning him into an idiot. If only he was old enough to have to go to school! Someone would come round looking out for him, then."

" There are inspectors," suggested Celia, firing up with indignation.

Mrs. Wicken froze. "We don't want anybody like that round here," she said.

She paused. "You're married, aren't you?" she asked.

"Yes," said Celia, in not at all the proud way she had been used to admitting it.

"Then tell your husband," urged Mrs. Wicken. "He might know what to do, without involving us. I wouldn't like to be the one to set officials and that lot on to the old lady. She took him in for the mother's sake, because she knew her as a girl, and now the mother's dead she's terrified of losing him. She's fond of him. It's just that she's too old now to have charge of a kid. She doesn't realise how long she sleeps, or how a boy ought to be running about. She treats him like a baby in arms. Now, if you'll excuse me, I shall have to go. I have to ride to my work, and it takes me best part of an hour."

THIRTY-TWO

MRS. WICKEN turned to the door, and Celia began to follow her. But when she saw Celia's backward glance, Mrs. Wicken stopped. "Why don't you stay with him a bit?" she suggested. "See if you can get him to laugh. I can tell you're worried. And the old lady won't be back for hours, I can promise you that."

" Perhaps I will. Just for a while," said Celia nervously.
Mrs. Wicken smiled, and went out.

Celia went slowly back and knelt down upon the dusty
rug. Johnny watched her. He was obviously surprised, but
he did not seem afraid. She spoke to him, but he did not
answer, and, after a moment, without knowing it, she fell
silent, staring into his face. No, he did not look like Larry.
But then, Larry's father, of whom she had seen a picture,
did not look like Larry, either.

The huge blue eyes blinked, and looked away. Celia
realised how hard she had been staring. " But I'm a mon-
ster!" she said to herself. " Kneeling down and glaring at a
child who's hardly seen me before! It's enough to frighten
him into fits."

She devoted herself then to feeding Johnny with the
jellybabies, chirruping to him, and trying to get him to
speak to her. But though he took the sweets as she offered
them, and watched her hopefully, she never coaxed a smile
from him. And gradually she grew frightened that Mrs.
Ryder would return and find her. And there was the ironing not done, and Larry's supper to prepare. She got up,
instinctively dusting herself down, and spoke firmly.

" I've got to go, now. Goodbye, Johnny," she said.

Johnny turned his head to watch her go to the door.
When her hand was on the door-knob he let out a devas-
tating howl. Celia hesitated, then snatched the door open,
and ran. It was no use. She could not stay, so why attempt
to console him? She would have to go in the end.

It was when she was hurrying home that Celia understood
for certain that she was pregnant. She had only had the dawn
of a hope before, but suddenly, as she walked back along
the lane, she was quite certain. Only a pathologist could

have told her, at that stage, but Celia knew. With her joy there came immense relief. For Larry would agree now that there could be no question of adopting a child. She would ask him to speak to Mrs. Ryder, and see that something was done for Johnny. But Johnny would not supplant their own children.

Celia sang as she did the ironing, made the pie for supper. Larry, who had taken to looking at her questioningly before he spoke, to gauge her mood, brightened up when he heard her as he came in. They had a gay and talkative meal, just like old times, and afterwards Larry helped wash up. It was while she was looking out of the kitchen window that Celia said dreamily,

" I suppose that porch we designed would be big enough for a pram?"

She expected Larry to guess. She expected him to lay down his tea-towel, as he did, and turn to her with surprise and fearful joy. But she did not expect what he said.

" Does that mean you'll have Johnny for a bit, then, if I can find him," he asked eagerly.

" No, never!" said Celia. She upturned the washing-up bowl with one angry movement, rinsed the dishcloth and threw it down, and went out of the room.

The same turmoil of indignation seized her as before. Larry did not care that it would be Johnny who called him Daddy, before their son could, who would be a step ahead of him all the way, skimming off the interest, the honour, that should have come to their own first-born. He thought only of Iris's child, and had not even guessed what Celia was trying to tell him. Now she would not tell him. Let him find out.

Larry stayed in the kitchen, clearing up, alone. Afterwards he went and worked in the garden. That was the pattern of all the week. He was very gentle with Celia, very considerate, but she knew that it was only to hide that he thought she had failed him. Celia said nothing to him about Mrs. Wickens's message. She was horrified at herself but she could not bring herself to speak of it.

Yet the next Monday afternoon saw her marching round to Mrs. Ryder's back door. There was no sign of Mrs. Wicken or Mrs. Ryder, but Johnny was there in the kitchen with his old coat wrapped around him. He knew Celia again, and greeted her with a slight uncertain smile.

It tugged at Celia's heart, but she scoffed at herself and him.

" And they say children can tell those who like them! " she exclaimed. " I'm not a friend, Johnny, do you hear? In fact, I don't know what I'm here for at all."

Johnny smiled again, and Celia was ashamed of herself. She peeled and quartered an apple from their own garden, and fed it to him. While he was eating, she undid the cord.

It was tied in a great many clumsy knots by old and stiffened fingers, but it gripped him tightly enough. At first Johnny did not seem to know what to do with his freedom, but Celia held out the end of her raincoat belt to him. He moved to grab it, she whisked it away, then let him catch and hold it. He chuckled, and waved it, then held it out to her again.

Johnny was playing! Celia had been afraid that he did not know how, and she was relieved and touched. He laughed and made a grab, and then got to his feet to catch at her waist. Then a dreadful thing happened. He stopped dead, and began to feel in a puzzled way behind him.

At first Celia did not understand. Then she did, and

was angrier than she had ever been in her life. Johnny was groping for the cord, afraid that if he tried to move too suddenly it would drag him down. " You poor little mite! " said Celia, and clutched him to her in a reassuring protective passion.

Johnny responded with a sound between a scream and a whimper. Celia held him away a little. His hands were on his stomach. She pulled up his grubby jersey, his grey vest, and saw a long raw place where the cord had chafed and chafed again.

At that moment Celia went a little mad. She snatched Johnny up again, not minding his considerable weight, though she felt it. She carried him to his old push chair, and put him in, added his beloved rabbit. Then, without a backward glance, she started off down the lane through the village.

She was about half way home before she hesitated, and then only for a second.

" She doesn't deserve to know where he is! " she exclaimed fiercely. " I'll tell Larry to go round when he gets back."

Celia wheeled Johnny into the cottage, and got to work. She bathed him and washed his hair, and cut it, and cut his nails, and bandaged the sore place. Then she wrapped him in an eiderdown while she washed his clothes, and dried them, even the shabby jersey and knickers, which she put round the fire to dry. The clothes were not so dirty as she had expected. They were grey all over, but only because they had been washed by someone who had not rinsed out the dirt. The sore was as bad as she had thought, however. Tonight Celia would show it to Larry, tomorrow take Johnny to the doctor.

Johnny did not know that he was being rescued. He had enjoyed the journey in his chair, looking around with every sign of interest. But he was still and quiet in Celia's house, bewildered by her actions and the strangeness. Celia thought that he was sometimes petrified with fear, and she worked harder than she had ever done in her life to soothe and distract him. She held him on an arm while she used the washer. She crooned, she rocked him on her lap, she gave him his dirty rabbit, and refrained from washing it or taking it out of his mouth when he sucked it, and while his clothes were drying she carried him into the garden all wrapped up, and showed him round. She never relaxed her efforts for a moment, and when she was quite exhausted had the reward of seeing him drop asleep with perfect confidence in her aching arms.

She slid him gently onto the settee in the sitting-room, and covered him up. She looked down at his sleeping face with real tenderness. He was like Larry! She could see it now. And she no longer resented it, but meant to accept and love him as if he had been Larry himself.

Larry came in with his questioning eyes. Celia did not give him time to take off his coat.

"Look," she said, and led him to Johnny. "I found him."

He did not seem so pleased as she expected, but she wasted no time. Gently she lifted the eiderdown, undid the rug, showed him the sore. Larry's face whitened with anger.

"He was with a Mrs. Ryder. He must never go back to her," said Celia fiercely.

"Mrs. Ryder!" exclaimed Larry. "But she was a Bailey! Victor Bailey's aunt! I ought to have known, when we talked about him, that Iris was putting me off."

" I think he'll be quite happy to stay," Celia said interrupting. " Now you must go and tell Mrs. Ryder where he is, and that we'll never give him back."

Larry seemed to hesitate.

" We'll all go," said Celia resolutely. " There's the pushchair to go back as well. You must buy me a better one as soon as you can."

Larry picked up the sleeping Johnny, who did not stir, and looked down at his face. Worriedly, not proudly, as a man should look at his son. Celia reached up and kissed him.

" I'm sorry I was so mean," she said. " Of course we'll keep him."

" You weren't mean," Larry told her. The sleeping child prevented him from kissing Celia back, but his expression told her what he felt.

They loaded themselves into the car, child in the back, push-chair on roof.

' For all the world like a family already,' thought Celia, with a smile to herself, and she hugged her own secret.

THIRTY-THREE

THERE WAS no one at the Ryders' when they went to the door. But, after a second, a man who must have been Mr. Wicken showed himself over the dividing hedge.

"Her's just coming now," he told them, and then disappeared again, before there could be trouble.

Mrs. Ryder stumped towards them along the path to her back door, head bent, very weary, but darting sour glances from side to side. Celia was sorry for her, but even more determined on her course. Then Mrs. Ryder looked up and turned a queer clay-colour. The car had not alerted her; she must have thought it was for the Wickens. She had not glanced inside, and she thought that Johnny was still tied up in the kitchen, and that the strangers had been waiting to see how long she would leave him alone. Then she recognised Larry, and, with dull surprise, Celia.

She said straightaway, "The bus went off without me, and I had to wait for the next," but shock and weariness had taken all the fight out of her. She listened when Larry told her that they had taken Johnny, and intended to keep him, and did not protest.

They left her staring after them as they marched down the path. By the car Mr. Wicken was now waiting.

He, unlike Mrs. Ryder, had had a good look inside, and he nodded at the sleeping Johnny.

"About time someone looked out for him," he said approvingly.

Larry's lips tightened angrily. Celia did the replying.

"He's going to stay with us," she said. "I dare say Mrs. Ryder will be upset about it, but it can't be helped. Do you think that your wife might keep an eye on her?"

Mr. Wicken looked doubtful, but said that his wife would see what she could do. His wife had an idea that Mrs. Ryder herself knew well enough that she was not equal to looking after a small child, but she had promised Johnny's mother, and was so pig-headed that she would not give up unless she was forced. But he would ask Mrs. Wicken to see what she could do. Celia felt that that might be a great deal, for Mrs. Wicken had energy and indignation. She had not wanted a row with a neighbour, but she would do everything she could, now.

They drove back to the cottage. Johnny still slept like an angel. Celia made Larry help her put up the spare bed for him in their room before she allowed him any supper. And while they were eating she was trying to decide whether she had to lift Johnny at ten o'clock, and what she ought to give him for his breakfast. Larry would not have been able to get a word in edgeways. But Celia knew that he was being quiet, and she was trying to reassure him by gaiety and chatter.

They went up again to see how Johnny was getting on, after they had washed up. He slept in a tight huddle, with a frown on his face, but it faded as Celia tucked the blanket more snugly.

Larry came behind her as she bent over the bed, and when she straightened kissed the back of her neck. They went downstairs with their arms round each other.

But when they were undressing that night some demon got into Celia.

" How often did you sleep with Iris?" she asked.

" How often . . .?" Larry's voice was outraged.

" Well, you must have slept with her," said Celia crossly.

" Naturally," he said stiffly.

" Was it only the once?"

Larry looked at her as if he could not believe his ears. " If it upsets you to think about it, wouldn't you do better not to ask?" he said. He was red in the face, and Celia could tell that he was upset. ' But it is I who have the right to be upset!' she said to herself angrily. 'And why shouldn't I know whether it was just once and they regretted it, or a real affair?' She kept silence, however.

When Larry got in to bed, with an upheaval, as she had often told him, like a herd of buffaloes at a water-hole, he lay stiffly beside her. But it was he who spoke first.

"You know," he said diffidently, "we may not be allowed to keep Johnny long. Even if we take him away from Mrs. Ryder, we may not be allowed to have him for good."

"They can't take him away from you. You are entitled to have him!" said Celia, rearing up.

"Iris wouldn't mind my having him now, I suppose," said Larry heavily. "I don't know how much that would count with Bill."

"How did it happen?" asked Celia. She spoke cautiously; keeping her demon in check.

"I was fond of Iris," said Larry. "I always had been. I was very sorry for her. Like a fool, I thought I could make things right. She never told me she was married."

"You were in love with her!"

"I thought so, I remember, at the time."

Celia's demon stirred again. "It's a pity for Johnny, though," she said coldly.

She got out, and went over to the spare bed.

"What are you doing?" asked Larry.

"Just making sure he's all right," she said. "If we adopted him legally," she went on, "would people have to know that he was illegitimate?"

"Johnny isn't illegitimate!" exclaimed Larry in an indignant voice. "If he hadn't been Bill Anslow's son, he would have been mine."

"But I don't understand," said Celia.

" I thought you said someone had written you a letter?"

" It didn't tell me anything like this! What happened, then?"

" Iris told us, when she came running to Mother, that she had been widowed. She must have believed Keith's story! As you know, Bill was very much alive. But Iris let me marry her three weeks later. We didn't tell Mother because we knew very well she would object. When Iris found she was pregnant, she told me at once that it must be her husband's child. He's John Anslow, and no more illegitimate than I am."

Larry seemed really cross that Celia had thought John was illegitimate. She was terrified now in case he guessed what else she had been thinking. She kept as quiet as a frightened mouse, and Larry went on,

" It was about a month after she told me that she was pregnant that Iris left me. Mother had heard someone mention Bill Anslow, and she spoke of him to Iris, though we didn't understand that was what had happened, at the time. Iris simply told me that we'd never been married at all, legally. She had been someone else's wife all the time, and the baby was his, too. I wasn't anything at all."

" How terrible for you," said Celia.

" I didn't take it very well," admitted Larry. " Perhaps it wasn't entirely Iris's fault, but, once I started, I un-covered other lies she had told me. I didn't love her any more, but I couldn't see anything else to do but to get her divorced, and then marry her again. But I felt I had a right to wait a little, and get my breath."

" Anyone would feel that way," said Celia loyally.

" Iris lost her temper. We had a row, and she rushed off. She wrote and said she never wanted to see me again. I said

Mother and I would look after her and the baby, but she said the baby was nothing to do with us, and she was determined never to let me or Mother get our hands on him.

" Mother was furious with me. She said she could have told me that nothing but trouble came of being sorry for Iris. Mother managed to find out from Maud that the baby had been safely born, and that it was a boy, and that Iris was paying to have him looked after by someone they knew in the old days. But she said Iris would make her life not worth living if she told Mother who and where. I didn't want to marry Iris again, so I gave up. Then I met you."

" Why didn't you tell me?"

" I meant to tell you. But I thought I ought to wait. Your own family seemed so blessedly uncomplicated, and you were so innocent. And I told myself that it was as if none of it had happened. Legally I hadn't ever been married before, and Johnny wasn't my son. And then, when we settled here, I got to wondering whether perhaps he might be, after all, and if that was the reason why Iris wouldn't let me or Mother get a look at him. She knew I didn't want to re-marry her, and she would never forgive that."

" If he's yours, we shall be able to tell," Celia prophesied, going to snuggle against him. " If he is, we'll keep him, even if Bill Anslow objects. But he won't. Flora won't let him."

She paused. "What sort of name will go well with Johnny?" she asked, deliberately making an effect. " Martin, perhaps? ' These are our little boys, John and Martin.' Yes, I think that would be nice."

THIRTY-FOUR

IT WAS a Saturday, and the first truly spring-like day, sunny, and with a warm wind. Larry, reviving from the exhaustion of the working week, proposed to make a bonfire of all the rubbish from the garden and some out of the loft. Johnny, quite at home now, ran in and out, under the impression that he was assisting. All of Celia's family was completely happy.

When the bonfire was well alight Bill Anslow stepped through the hedge to speak to Larry. Presently he went away, and came back bearing Maudie the dressmaker's shape, soiled and streaked from her long sojourn on the rubbish heap, among the chervil and cowparsley.

Flora had consented that Maudie should be burned, Bill announced. She wouldn't have her in the house; she wouldn't let Bill put her out for the dustmen. Now she had at last agreed that she should be burned, though not in Bill's own garden.

Celia did not hear what Bill said. The first she knew about his intention was when he and Larry between them picked Maudie up, and laid her fair and square across the flame. The pink kid darkened at once, and began to smell vilely. The shape seemed to writhe, more human now than ever.

One end curled up, and Celia gave a scream. Even Bill and Larry were impressed, and Larry hastily pushed with the rake to press Maudie down into the flames.

He must have caught some invisible seam. There was a brief gleam, and then a stream of gold, ninety-eight golden sovereigns, shone palely for a moment as they shot out into the real gold of the fire's heart.

Larry sprang on the bonfire, kicking at the brands, raking, spreading out. Bill feverishly assisted him. Johnny laughed and jumped about. Larry turned and lifted him to the wall of the pigsty run, out of harm's way. Bill turned to keep an eye on him.

Celia stood transfixed. Johnny's profile, she saw, was side by side with Bill's, as they paused for a moment, gazing at the blackened debris. Johnny's face, still soft and blobby, was yet recognisably Bill's. The two had exactly the same expression, mouth slightly open in intense surprise, eyes vacant.

" Oh, Johnny! " Celia said.

With all her heart she apologised to him.

" I'll love you just as much. In fact I'll love you more," she promised silently, " I'll love you more, for not being Larry's son."